WELCOM
GOA

Goats are strong-willed and unpredictable. They chew through armoured cables, slip under fences and, inexplicably, end up on rooftops. Nonetheless, goats uphold their own definition of grace. They can stand for many hours on the side of a mountain, sure-footed amongst the boulders and scree, their gaze trained on the sun setting behind some distant hill. Goats are loyal, yet fiercely independent. You can tell each goat apart by the way it lifts its chin to face the oncoming wind.

The Goatshed is shelter and communion. It is for people who believe in Art as Play, as the domain of the trickster, a space not defined by duty, but the crackle of possibility. At Goatshed Press we aim to deliver exciting, unpretentious content while discovering and uplifting a new generation of writers and artists.

This collection is made possible due to the dedication and hard work of a lot of people; writers, editors, sculptors, designers, painters, printers and proofreaders, who have come together to form a kind of emergent collective, a Goatshed Family, each living a different life in a different place, yet united by attitude, each stood atop their own mountain, chins braced against the oncoming wind.

Remember, this is only the beginning.

Goatshed One

Published by Goatshed Press, Great Britain, 2023

Work published with permission from the writers, who retain the right to be indentified as the authors of their work

Art is, either, published with permission from the artist or taken from the public domain

Designed by Jack Jenkins and David Humphries

Printed by KOPA

www.goatshedpress.co.uk

CONTENTS

A Nearby Town

Julian Harvard

They'd taken a villa in a dead olive grove looking over a town of white cubes that burned orange whenever the sun came down. They were close enough to hear its church bells and the teenagers who drank in the piazza, the Vespas that grumbled up and down its worn cobbles. Close enough to touch, far enough to feel apart.

Alice and Tom had been in Italy a week and the sun hadn't relented. It battered the stone walls and shrivelled the grapes on the vines. Dark cracks had formed in the earth between the dead trees, across the sea of baked clay that surrounded them, and there was a fine red dust that hung in the air and powdered the surfaces. They could feel it on their teeth and between their toes. It settled on the sweaty soft flesh behind their knees. The land was suffering and, when a maestrale howled, the trees and earth seemed to scream in reply.

'Forty-four fucking degrees,' Tom said, jabbing his phone excitedly.

Officially the hottest he had been in his thirty-eight years. 'How about that?'

Alice rolled away from him and took a long, lazy sip from her negroni. She looked out over the pool as the sparrows dive-bombed for water.

'Global warming is a tragedy beyond anything humanity has ever known,' she said as if she didn't mean it.

'It's weather, Alice. And we're in a hot country. Everything here is designed for heat.'

Alice noticed a black snake, half as long as her lounger, emerge from the pool's pump, bask for a second in the sun, then disappear into a gap in the stone wall that separated them from the olive grove.

'What about the dead trees? They don't seem designed for it,' she said.

'It's a virus, baby. Not sure you can put that on Big Oil or Ryanair.'

Every olive tree for miles around had died, withered by Xylella disease. Graveyards of gnarled trunks and bare branches stretched endlessly in every direction. It could have been winter were it not for the heat and the mosquitoes. Disquieting at first, Alice and Tom had quickly grown used to it. Eventually, the world beyond their villa had dissolved out of focus, along with the names of days and the gnawing anxieties of home.

They were now well settled into the holiday rhythm. Hangovers had ceased and in their place came a constant coddling fog that clouded their thoughts and maintained good tempers. The days had taken on a metronome beat: pool, drink, lounger, lunch, drink, bed, pool, lounger, drink. They would welcome the night with a Prosecco and a bowl of olives. Then sloppy pasta and Primitivo by the carafe.

At the start of the holiday, as she did every year, Alice had protested at Tom's enthusiasm for the foreign liquor aisle. She had blushed in the supermarket as he trailed the auxiliary drinks trolley behind the food trolley, as he slapped the first gallon bottle onto the belt with a grin and a cry of 'Grande festa!' Whether the girl had really curled her lip and raised her eyebrows hardly mattered; Alice still felt an intense shame at their indulgence. Sorry, she had wanted to say. Sorry we are such rich, greedy locusts, such grotesque aliens, linen-clad and pale-skinned and red-cheeked. Sorry for his boat shoes, sorry for the absurd brim of my hat, my seven-hundred pound hemp handbag. Sorry, so very sorry. But instead she had smiled demurely and busied herself with packing. Eventually, as ever, she would settle into Tom's slipstream and keep pace.

Tom rolled onto his back and burped. Alice sensed his weight behind her, the struggle to lift the belly up and over, the creak of slats. Sometimes he revolted her. When they'd met it had seemed impossible that he would ever be anything other than beautiful. His angularity, those sharp cheeks, that tousled hair; his looks had been so strong as to seem eternal, and he possessed something in his spirit that diluted his acerbity, a kindness almost, even if only she could see it. But now she could find that beauty nowhere, not even in his eyes, within which something had extinguished. People degraded, she knew that; her sense of entropy was as strong as her sense of temperature, of pain. And yet, where Tom had succumbed happily to age soon after their marriage, she had committed to staying exactly as she was. Her regime punished her. The early mornings, her vile personal trainer, the endless, excruciating denial of pleasure. She envied Tom's capitulation but so wished he had fought alongside her for longer. Instead, he had bolted from their trench to be gunned down just beyond it. His corpse was peaceful, its stench constant.

'Christ, he's here again. Il contadino.' Tom was peering over his Ray-Bans into the olive grove where a small man stepped between the trees. His skin was brown and wrinkled, tough and craggy, as if he had absorbed and retained all the sun that had ever shone on him. He tapped a trunk with his fingers and put his ear against the bark as if listening for signs of life.

8

'They're dead. Give it up mate,' Tom muttered.

'Let him be. There's probably never been a day in his life where he hasn't tended these olives. And now there's nothing left.'

'He should retrain. We need fewer olive farmers, more computer repairmen and Bitcoin miners.'

Alice let herself laugh. Tom, satisfied, hauled himself up and launched into the pool, his swallow dive aborting mid-flight into a belly flop. He proceeded to clamber onto a lilo and float face down, singing Sinatra.

Alice ignored him and watched the farmer as he walked between the trees, tapping and listening. From a bag at his side he pulled out a small olive branch, thick with leaves, their greenness loud as a foghorn in the grey grove. With a chisel he carved notches into a sawn trunk and, by the time he had finished, five new branches had been inserted into the old tree. To Alice it looked utterly futile, a child's solution to a problem without one. Pity overwhelmed her and she felt like crying. To be so committed to a life that would not return. What a way to live, she thought.

Tom roused her with a splash from the pool and exhorted her to join him. She relented. The heat had become too much to bear and as she jumped in and the water took her she felt, for the briefest moment, born anew.

"Alice!'

'Alice!'

Tom called from somewhere.

Alice was in bed. She had been in a deep sleep. The sky through the open balcony door was black but starting to soften.

'Alice!'

She turned over. He could get like this, drink firing him up as he slept, sending him from nightmares into waking panic. She felt awful, blood thick, head heavy. They had stayed up late drinking and bickering and she hadn't been asleep long enough to blunt the edges of the alcohol or defuse the cotton-mouthed sourness. She drifted off but, when she woke next, Tom was by the bed, shaking her. He was naked, his pot belly sweaty and reflective, his eyes wild.

'Alice. Alice. Wake up.'

'Breathe, Tom.'

'Please. Get up.'

She could see him clearly now. Was he crying?

'Tom?'

'There's something happening. Over town — I went for a piss and — I don't understand. Alice please.'

She had seen him like this before: as a drunken, bloodied boy, two months into their relationship, standing outside her parents' door in the early hours, mugged, desperate for her embrace. Or the day, two years ago, she had discovered his affair, small and meaningless as he claimed it was, when he'd cried into her lap for so long that she had said sorry. So, again, she would have to be stronger than him, whatever had happened. Her head ached terribly.

'Darling, it'll be alright. Get back to bed.'

'There's something happening to the town. There's something over it.'

'You're drunk still —'

'I can see it in the church lights. Moving just slightly. Something, Alice. A thing. You're not listening! I am wide awake.'

The sky was paler. The room had become blue and ghostly.

'Let me sleep, then I'll —'

'You have to see. Come and look. Alice!' He tugged at her arm. She groaned and allowed herself to be pulled from bed. Tom stumbled back to the balcony and she approached him slowly, studying his face. It was full of such wonder and fear that he seemed to be someone else, more like a child. It sobered her.

'Tom. This is silly.' But now she was outside and she could see what he saw. Above the town, hovering still and silent, an amorphous black mass from which appendages hung limply. As large as the town itself, it seemed to be made only of muscled, scaly flesh. A rotted vegetal stench filled the air. She grasped for an anchor, a memory, some knowledge that could place this thing in the natural order, but she was cut loose. She knew it was no dream. The world against her skin was too solid, the warmth of the air, the hardness of the stone under her feet. This thing was as real as everything she knew, as organic as the snake on the wall or the millipedes in the plant pots — and yet, it was something other. She traced the thing from the thin tip of one of its extremities and up its tentacles. There were nine of them. She saw that they swayed in the breeze and each stopped just shy of the buildings. The spotlights on the campanile lit the thing's undercarriage, revealing the definition between its scales, each one as large as the bell in the tower, as smooth as marble. She tuned in to the screams that drifted up from the town, engines roaring, dogs howling, glass smashing. Headlights and tail lights flashed through distant trees. A siren sounded somewhere.

'What do we do?' Tom asked.

The question was farcical to Alice. Unanswerable. He looked so pitiful, standing naked in the wake of whatever this was, exposed with his wild wiry pubic hair, his penis lit blue in the dawn light.

'We should run, we need to get away,' he said, but she wouldn't answer. She had resolved not to. She turned back to the thing. It hovered so inertly, with such little intent. It was like a dead fish floating in the shallows. Surely there was menace, surely this thing would descend wreak destruction. But, for as long as it didn't, Alice could not fear it.

Tom ducked back inside and static crackled from the radio that grew louder or quieter as he turned the dial. He emerged with his phone.

'No signal. No internet. No radio. We have to leave.'

'But look, Tom...' she pointed into the distance. The sky had brightened and on the horizon hung black shapes. 'Every village, every town. But nothing over us.'

'We need to pack —'

'But we're safe here, Tom, I think that's quite clear. Where would we go?' She gripped him firmly on the arm. 'Why don't you make us breakfast?'

Tom went limp but she fixed him with a gaze of such strength that it seemed to straighten him. He backed away into the house, covering his genitals with his hands.

'What are they, Alice?' He asked from inside. Alice shrugged and leaned on the railings.

'I think they're nothing to worry about, Tom. They're far away.'

They had a breakfast of honeyed toast, wine and coffee on the balcony and watched the thing as the sun rose and exposed it in all its blackness. It didn't move. Its musty fetor drifted in and out as the winds changed and eventually they became inured to it.

By noon the strength of the sun, hotter than it had been all week, forced them down to the pool. Tom was subdued. He had given up speculating on what the thing might be. All his theories — the secret weaponry of a hostile state, products of a shared hallucination — had been ignored by Alice. He took compulsive sips of his drink rather than his big, hoggish gulps. He could not keep his eyes from the thing in the sky. Occasionally he suggested that they leave but Alice dismissed him. She had, by now, developed only a detached interest in the thing, glancing at it every now and then, as if it were a rainbow or a lightning storm.

In the afternoon the brittle grasses of the olive grove caught fire. Enough, they seemed to say, the heat was too much. When the farmer appeared, Tom bounded up to speak with him.

'Cos'e, cos'e?' Tom demanded, pointing wildly at the black thing over town. The farmer battled the flames with old rugs but soon the dead trees caught fire too. He began clearing a ring around the grafted olive tree. He flapped at Tom to leave him alone. 'I think he knows what it is, Alice! He's being a slippery fucking prick.'

But Alice didn't care. She went into the house to

fetch the bottle of Franciacorta they had been keeping in reserve for their last night. Emerging back onto the terrace, she popped the cork and watched as it looped into the hot hazy sky.

'Come on, Tom. Have a drink.' She poured their glasses. Tom, under her spell, shuffled over and took up the glass. Alice chinked hers against his and turned toward the town. It was quiet now. It must have emptied. She imagined some remaining old women, defiant, clinging to their homes, reasoning that they had seen worse, and where would they go anyway now the whole world was under siege?

'Alice, are you sure we shouldn't go? The consulate will help us.'

'Let's stay until we are made to leave.'

Tom nodded, by now so eager to be led that he didn't care where. Alice knocked back her drink and wiped the liquid from around her mouth. The smoke was billowing over the pool, the farmer caught between fight and retreat as he worked to protect the grafted tree. Alice's heart broke for him once again, but she was now hotter than she had ever been and she could only think of the pool and its cool water. She dived in, dispersing the fine ashy layer that floated on top. She sank to the bottom and kept herself there, cross-legged. She opened her eyes and through the water above she saw the undefined black vision of her husband and the clouds of smoke upon him. She resolved to stay in the water until she could stand it no more.

A Walk with My Father in '29

That day the sun had a funeral shawl around her
and I was a man and my father
was a boy; we were a blur
and the road smelt of rotten cassava

Son, walk with me to the yam barn
let me show you a painting of my grandma, for
a child sent by his father to steal breaks down the door

And trudge, we trudged, my father and I hand in hand
one thousand nine hundred and twenty-nine miles to our
yam barn
just behind our kindred hut and
it was the year my father's white coat tenant became our
landlord over our heads and threatened to evict us from
our ancestral land

Son, the first time I saw grandma she was naked,
but her legs shut to the world
and one of our kinsmen had become a messenger
to an alien vulture my grandfather
blessed with a shelter
a vulture that came gaunt and terrified of mosquitoes
a vulture with white blemishes

Just so you know,
my great-grandmother had only two goats and two
chickens
and two cowards — my grandfather one of them, quick
to fold

Just so you know,
we knew no kings and queens
every man is a king and his wife a queen in their
household

Just so you know,
so we lived until the arrival of the white feathered
vultures
so that the year when the road was
nineteen thousand and twenty-nine miles long,
a mere messenger came by my great-grandmother's hut
taxing for her goats and chickens —
and not for the coward she kept and fed —

a walk all over her nakedness,
bruising not her body but her soul and dignity

Just so you know,
her voice, oiled and cooking,
she became thunder and lightning —
she cried to the sun and the sea —
and in three nights,
all the women from across the regions
of the earth converged and walked barefoot
in flowing white robes all over our lands

Just so you know,
they raised so much dust the land went on its knees,
our landlord lost some of his fat

> *Son, sit with me for a while,*
> *this world is no place for tired bones,*
> *sit with me for a while,*
> *for a forest that provides*
> *a child with firewood must also provide him with the*
> *ropes*
> *for bundling it. You must watch for slopes*

Perch we perched on the brown earth,
our lungs battling carbon monoxide from wretched men,
our skin responding to an angry December harmattan

vultures flying over our heads on their way to English
heaven,
yapping hunger and thirst

Son, our god is a woman
never forget that where a child is given yam the first
time
he'll return to a second time
never bite your god's finger
don't be a man of easy timber
for not every road leads to the heart of a brave woman

And up we stood, but he fell
it was the last time my father would stand on his feet
we never made it to the yam barn
today I say to his silhouette,
if a child washes his hands clean,
he will dine with gods.

Michael Ndubuisi Agugom

Alex Kanevsky

Alex Kanevsky was born in the Soviet Union in 1963. He studied mathematics at Vilnius University in Lithuania before coming to the United States. After his arrival in Philadelphia in 1983 he worked as Russian translator, illustrator at the Psychiatric Nursing Magazine, and drew pictures for telephone book advertisements. After attending PAFA (1989-93) and winning a Pew Fellowship (1997) he devoted himself to painting full time. Alex Kanevsky lives and works in New Hampshire. He has exhibited his work in the United States, Canada, Italy, UK, France, Spain, Ireland and Japan. His work is represented by Hollis Taggart in New York and Dolby Chadwick Gallery in San Francisco.

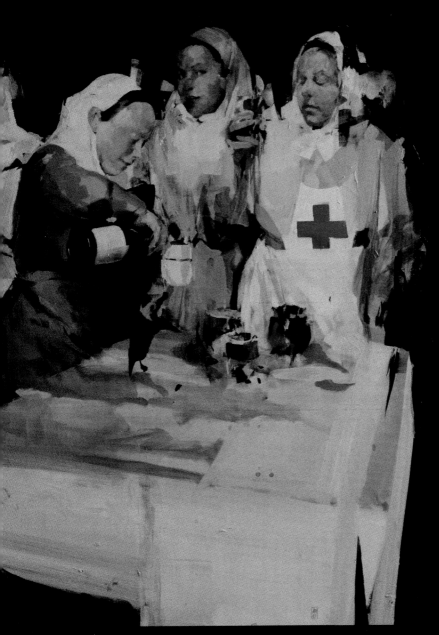

Jan Kopeusky   Nurses With Wine

Alex Kanevsky —

Postcards from a Closet

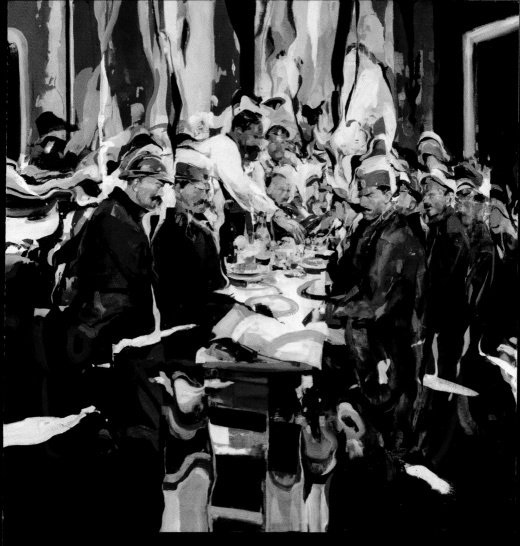

Alex Kanevsky — *Dinner on a Battlefield*

Alex Kanevsky — *Dear Friend*

Lodger

Maddy Docherty

You meet Alistair on a Sunday afternoon. You: catastrophically hungover after a night of solo drinking, keenly aware of your smoky hair and smudged makeup. Him: early, nervous and alone, despite the Facebook ad specifying a room in the house of a married couple. 'I'm away a lot and my wife hates being in the house by herself,' he says, and he struggles to meet your gaze for more than a few seconds, eyes darting around the room as he drinks his espresso. You sip your peppermint tea, grimacing, taking deep breaths to keep the nausea at bay. 'You might know

her actually, she's a poet. Well, she has a book of poems.'
When he says her name you don't recognise it, but pretend
you do, and he smiles at you, giving you the impression
that you have passed a test you didn't know you were
taking. After a few more stilted questions you exchange
phone numbers and part ways. You catch the bus back
to your flat and get straight into bed fully clothed. When
your ex-boyfriend gets home from work he comes into the
bedroom and asks if you're okay, if you're feeling better.
You ignore him, head under the covers and, after a minute,
you hear the bathroom door close and the shower switch
on. You don't think you're going to hear back about the
room but, a few weeks later, you do.

   You move in fast, without viewing the room first,
and when you call your mother to tell her your change of
address she sounds worried. 'Are you sure this is the right
thing to do? When you're still so, fragile?' You suspect
that she's been talking to your ex, and you can almost
hear the pity in their voices as they discuss what they're
going to do about you. You reassure her that a fresh start
is exactly what you need and when she hangs up you
dig your fingertips into your palms until you carve small
crescents in your skin. When you arrive at the address
that Alistair sent you your Uber driver helps you unload
your possessions onto the drive. He straightens his back

and stretches his arms before looking up at the house and letting out a low whistle. When you ring the doorbell a woman answers and, you think, the wife.

You're the same height and you get the sense that she is older than you, though she doesn't look it. She is clearly younger than her husband. You have the same haircut but hers looks expensive, her full fringe cut razor straight where yours is jaggy and done yourself with kitchen scissors. She's wearing paint-stained overalls with knitted socks and Birkenstocks, like a caricature of an artist. She introduces herself and tells you that you can bank transfer Alistair the rent, but if you ever need anything you're to ask her. Then she says, 'Oh, and your room is in the turret.' You repeat back to her, 'The turret?' and she looks embarrassed. 'It's round the back of the house, you won't have seen it from the driveway.' You follow her inside and along the corridor, trailing your hand along a dark wood mantelpiece with a huge Victorian-looking clock. When you lift your hand your fingertips come away dusty. She points you up a set of spindly stairs and doesn't follow you up or offer to help with your boxes. It takes you three trips to carry everything and, when you get to your room, it's cold and almost empty except for a bed and a gold-edged mirror leaning against the wall. You dump your bags and look out the small round window into the garden which is completely overgrown with plants and trees. You watch two squirrels race each other up the trunk of a thick, tall tree for a few seconds and then lie on the bed on top of the faded blanket and think, I am completely alone. You imagine her moving around the house below you in her socks and slippers. The thought feels comforting and you lie there for a few minutes, listening to the pipes gurgling, before falling asleep fully clothed. When you open your eyes the air in the room is still and it has become evening.

The next morning you get up and put a hoodie over your thin pyjama top before making your way downstairs to the kitchen. She is sitting at the table, reading, and looks up when you walk in. She looks confused for a moment, as if she has forgotten you live here now, but then she smiles and motions to the cafetiere in front of her on the table. It's early morning but she is already dressed in a cable-knit jumper and faded jeans, casual but expensive. You will yourself not to think about your holey leggings and university hoodie and, instead, you grab a wonky ceramic mug that's drying by the sink, pour yourself a cup of coffee, and sit down opposite her. You look at each other shyly. 'I like this,' you say, holding up the mug and she smiles and says, 'I made it myself,' before going back to her book. You drink the coffee and look around, wishing that you had something to read. The cupboards and cabinets are all mismatched in a way that only rich people can get away with. There's an antique looking cabinet against one of the walls which houses a dozen painted china plates. They're old fashioned and ugly, painted with floral patterns. You look at them, wondering how much they cost, and she pipes up, 'I didn't make those ones,' and when you look at her she's smiling back at you, eyebrows slightly raised. The next morning you come down to the kitchen again, a book in your hand, and she is in the same seat, the cafetiere on the table in front of her. She nods approvingly and you sit in comfortable silence, reading together for an hour or so before she snaps her book shut and says, 'right, better get going.' You hear her quiet steps make their way along the hall and into her office. You hear a door close and a few minutes later, muffled classical music makes its way under the gap in the door and into the kitchen.

Over the next few weeks you carve out a routine together. Coffee and reading at the kitchen table early every morning before she retreats to her office and you explore the streets surrounding the house. You walk for a few hours every day then return and wander around the rooms, inspecting dusty photographs of her and Alistair and placing them back in the same position. She doesn't seem to fit in the house, which is old fashioned and drab, and you are dying to have a look round her office, which you have decorated in your mind with colourful art pieces and trinkets collected on trips around the world. You eat lunch together and take it in turns to prepare the food, salad or eggs or cheese toasties. She does all of the food shopping and won't let you contribute financially or see the lists. As the weeks pass she starts buying you little treats, a bottle of wine or an expensive brand of yoghurt you mentioned that you liked. She asks you questions about your life and you give her the edited highlights. Once, you try to ask her about writing and she shuts you down saying 'No writing is getting done at the moment. That is the extent of the news.' You feel that, by asking, you have broken an unspoken rule between the two of you. When it gets dark you get ready for work at the bar, changing into tight jeans and t-shirt, overdoing your eyeliner and waving your hair. The first time she sees you like this she says 'Wowza!' and you shrug, your face burning. You work until the early hours of the morning, taking the night bus home and falling into bed past two most nights. When you arrive back at the house it is always dark and quiet, the dishes from dinner left to soak in the sink, the worktops littered with crumbs and stains. You find it difficult to maintain your early coffee mornings alongside your nocturnal job, but you feel like this domestic routine is fragile, that you are still a visitor in her home. You do your best to slip into her life like a stone into a lake, without a sound, ripples spreading across the surface. Unconsciously, you stop staying at the bar for post-shift drinks and start leaving as soon as you finish, eager to return home.

On your nights off you have dinner together and drink wine at the kitchen table. These nights are when you really talk, although your intuition tells you to steer away from certain topics. You don't bring up the fact that Alistair is never there, or that neither of you seem to have any friends. On these nights it's easy to pretend that you are the only two people in the world, that your universe goes no further than the kitchen table. You map out your lives before you met and marvel at the places your paths cross. You compare your semi-detached homes and overbearing single mothers. Every now and again you come up against a vast difference, something that overshadows the previous similarities and seems to send your individual lifelines spinning away from each other irretrievably. You find out that she met Alistair at university, while she was a student, and that he was already married to another professor in his department. She starts to tell you about the affair but you cut her off and change the subject as quickly as possible, hating the way her eyes light up when she says his name.

You ask her about the book, too tipsy by now to remember that she doesn't like talking about her writing, and she looks sad, so you tell her that you've read it, and you loved it, even though you haven't. She blushes and says, 'Oh my god I hate that you've read it.' You ask her how she got it published and she brushes the question away, saying that it was complicated and she could hardly remember. Later that night, red wine staining your lips and tongue, you google her name and the third result, under her author website and a link to purchase the book, is an online article about nepotism in the publishing industry. You slam your laptop shut before you can read anymore.

You find yourself living for these nights with her, for the expensive wine that you can't afford and the conversations that dart and weave from one story to the next. You tell her about getting your period when you were ten, the first in your class, about how your mother took you to the doctor and he gave you tablets to try and delay puberty, how it didn't work and your body changed shape rapidly, dimples spreading across your thighs and alien breasts straining against your training bra. You speak quickly as you tell her this, your face feeling hot and exposed in the dull kitchen light. She pays you back by telling you about the abortion she had when she was eighteen, how she got pregnant the first time she ever had sex and took herself to the clinic a few weeks after, alone, trying not to cry in front of the nurse. You ask her if she ever thinks about the baby and she says no, her tone dismissive. Later that night she is a little too drunk and you spin around the kitchen as you teach her a Scottish country dance you learned in school. Her hand fits neatly into yours and you hold it tight, playing the role of the man, twirling her around in messy circles and preparing to catch her if she falls.

The day after your kitchen ceilidh you come downstairs and she is putting red lipstick on, guided by her phone camera. She is dressed in feminine clothes, an obvious departure from her usual dungarees and knitwear. You notice that she's wearing heels. You greet her and she starts a little, smudging her cupid's bow and wiping off the red with her fingers. 'I'm meeting Alistair for brunch in town, he's back for a day but can't stay over.' Her eyes are bright and a little manic. She chats to you as she reapplies and you find yourself staring at her, not listening to what she's saying. She reaches out and grabs your hand, kissing your knuckles quickly to blot her lipstick and your whole body stiffens in response. She pulls back and grins at you, teeth bared, and says, 'Am I okay?' You can't speak. She repeats, 'My teeth, am I okay?' and you nod before you process what she's saying and then you come back to earth and say, 'Wait no.' You wipe the speck of red off her teeth with your finger, touching her enamel as gently as you can. You are unbelievably aware of your closeness and your breath catches a little, your stomach dropping with a pang of desire. In that second you feel like you are carved in her image, your body a poor imitation of hers, your teeth yellowing at the edges when viewed beside her sparkling whites. She runs her tongue over her teeth and says, 'Did you get it?' and you feel like she knows what you're thinking, feel like she can feel your pulse. You say, 'Yeah that's better,' and then you are both silent for a moment, looking at each other. Her phone buzzes with a text and she looks at it then says 'Oh, he cancelled.' Her voice is small. You say 'Who cares about him,' and she looks at you oddly then gets up and leaves the room. You don't see her for the rest of the day. The next morning you get dressed quickly and rush downstairs to see her, but the kitchen is empty. You look around for the cafetiere, planning to have everything ready for when she comes in, but you can't find it, and when you walk past her office the smell of fresh coffee fills your nose.

You start talking to her in your head, asking her questions and telling her about your dreams. Your life becomes an exercise in killing time until she comes back to you. You drift around the big supermarket at the end of the road, looking at the yellow stickers on the reduced food. You pick up cut-price salmon, brie, chocolate mousse, and put them all into your basket with vague ideas of cooking for a change, surprising her with dinner. It occurs to you that you have barely left the house, except to go work, in weeks. You can't remember when you stopped walking in the mornings. You watch a woman push a pram down the aisle towards you. She is talking on the phone and her eyes dart left and right, methodically scanning the shelves. The baby is a girl, about one, and her eyes flick back and forth too, mimicking her mothers, her eyes full of wonder as she surveys the brightly coloured products all around her. She reaches her chubby fist out, clutching at a pot of yoghurt, and her mother pauses her conversation to smack her hand away. The little girl starts to cry and before you know it you are standing beside the pram, holding the woman's wrist tightly. 'What are you doing?' she says to you, eyes wide with shock. 'Let her have the yoghurt,' you say quietly. 'She wants it.' You let go of her arm and lean down to the baby, who is filling the air with her screams. Before you can say anything else the woman jerks the pram away and starts hurrying back up the aisle. She looks back to make eye contact with you and you can see that she is afraid.

You abandon your basket at the entrance and rush

back to the house, chastising yourself for leaving in case she has been wondering where you are. On the walk home you decide that it is time to ask her what's going on, time to push her to admit to herself what she feels for you. When you walk into the hallway you can tell immediately that the house is empty. There are no keys on the mantelpiece and her coat is gone from the hook. Everything is silent except for the long slow ticks of the clock. You stand in the hallway for a long moment before you realise that your phone is ringing and when you check it you see that it is Alistair. You decline the call and walk slowly along the hallway and up the spindly staircase to your room, trying not to jump to conclusions. Your things have been neatly packed away into the cardboard boxes that you arrived with and the bedsheets have been stripped. You take off your shoes and coat, lie down on the uncovered mattress and close your eyes. You breathe in the fresh air coming through the open window and wait for her to come home.

Frozen Pond

Maddy Docherty

You call his landline like you did when you were kids, using the secret code: dial, let it ring three times, hang up, call back. His mother answers and it surprises you and you say 'Hey!' brightly then, remembering your circumstances, you repeat, 'Hey,' quieter, sombre. You pause and hear her take a breath in, like she's about to speak, but before she can you say 'Do you remember when the pond froze over so we asked you if we could go ice skating and you said no because you didn't have any skates?' The line is quiet so you keep talking, worried if you pause again she'll hang

up. 'We were only half-asking really, too old to show any enthusiasm, pretending that we didn't care. It was frozen right through, the pond I mean, I don't think I had ever seen it like that before. People were coming through from the West End to skate and some of them were really good. Fancy boots, proper snow gear and everything. I remember there was a little girl there every day, younger than us, with her dad. She would skate big loops around the pond and her dad would take photographs of her with a fancy camera. All the other skaters would give her space because she was so good. We used to watch her and I would be so jealous, kind of hoping she would fall. Sometimes she would draw a proper crowd, mums and old people and stuff.

We would sit on the bench, snow turning to water, bums soaked, and stare at her. Sometimes she would skate into the middle of the ice and do spins or jumps and I could feel everybody draw breath, waiting for the ice to break. I don't think she ever fell though; I think I would remember. Did you know that you only ever actually remember something properly once? Every subsequent remembering is just you remembering remembering, if that makes sense? That's what all my memories of me and him as kids are like, kind of blurry round the edges. I remember some things so clearly though, although I guess that will fade too, as I get older. And he — anyway. For those few frozen days we would watch everyone skate and sit on the bench and eat penny sweets from the shop, but we only ever went on the ice once.

We were messing about in the park, not just me and him, five or six of us, and it felt like it was really late, but it wasn't, not even dinnertime, you know how early it gets dark in the winter. And it gets so quiet that it feels like the middle of the night. We weren't really allowed in the park when it was dark because there weren't any streetlights — there still aren't, can you believe it? Somebody got stabbed there a few weeks ago and I thought, Jesus, no wonder you never wanted us in the park at night. But we used to go anyway and mess about in the playground or sit on benches and smoke, if someone had stolen their parents' cigarettes. And it's not like my mum ever cared where I was, so we just had you to lie to. Did you know what we were getting up to? Don't answer that.

That night we were waiting outside the supermarket, pooling our coins and asking people to buy us cider. I was always the one who had to ask because I always had the least change. Everyone hid round the corner and I hung about by the entrance, ready to run off if the man on the door noticed me. I asked this old guy if he would buy me some booze and he said yes, what kind? I said it didn't matter and then he came out with a plastic bag full of bottles. I could hear them clinking. And he gave me the bag and asked me what I was going to do with the drink and could he come and share it with me? and I panicked and ran away and when we got to the park and opened the bag, he'd bought me three bottles of red wine. And I remember feeling all mixed up about it, like I could tell he was lonely but also definitely a bit weird? And we drank the wine in the park, and it was so disgusting. I still don't like red wine much now but when you're thirteen, God, it is just minging. Warm red wine out the bottle in a freezing cold park by all the dog shit? No thanks. And everyone was teasing me and calling the guy a paedo and it made me feel sad.

Anyway, the pond, the frozen pond. We were messing about and then everyone had to go home for their dinner and I think he could tell that I was feeling left out and that nobody was at home for me, so he said, let's go to the pond. So, we went, shuffled onto the ice and slid right into the middle and lay down next to each other. It was absolutely freezing, so it was a stupid thing to do, but I had just seen The Notebook and I was obsessed with the bit where Ryan Gosling and Rachel McAdams both lie down next to each other in the road. Looking back that was such a sweet thing for him to do, wasn't it? Notice that I didn't want to go home. He was always doing things like that.

So, I was looking up at the moon and it was so white. I know that sounds stupid, but it looked like it was white all the way through. It made me feel even colder to look at it, two thirds full and glowing like teeth in American films. I remember we were holding hands and just being quiet together and then I said, I want to make sculptures when I'm older. And he said, oh yeah? And I said yeah, look at the moon right now. I pointed with my other hand. I want to make something physical, something that will stay forever. And he laughed and said you sound like such a wank, but then he squeezed my hand and after a minute he turned onto his side so I could see his whole face and said, that's cool.

I can see his face, how it looked then, shining, lit by the moon. His big front teeth and the pointy ones at the side, his freckles. He always looked so clean — soft hair and ironed clothes, although I know that was due to your hard work, not his. When the articles came out, after it happened, they made it seem like he was common, like he was dirty. I would hear people whisper about him in the supermarket when they saw me and I wanted to say, you never saw him like I saw him, shining in the moonlight, so close to the ice, entertaining my dreams. I know you aren't supposed to say this, but it shouldn't have been him that died. It isn't fair.

Oh god, sorry. My husband is calling me because I left the water boiling. I was listening to the radio and the news guy said there was going to be snow tomorrow and I just started thinking about him, about that winter. So, I called you on my mobile, you never forget your friend's house numbers, eh? I'm in the garden now. I wandered out while I was talking. I'm staring at the flowers at the end of the grass, the violas. They were here before we were and we haven't touched them. They're just there, blooming, in spite of us. When I was growing up, when I thought about the flat, or about mum, I never felt love, I never felt at home. I felt at home with him.'

You stop talking and for a moment there's just quiet at the end of the line and then you hear her exhale, heavily, like she's been holding her breath the whole time.

moons

though words are just fingers
pointing at the moon
let us raise all our fingers
for there are many moons
carved and distant
each one gleaming
in a restless sky
and I want to see them all
before I die

Duncan Richardson

knives, inward

sounded like the ghost of
laughter up on burnt hill rd

felt like being in love with you at 17

holy
but not stoned

       stoned
but not bleeding enough to
make any difference and it was this man i
worked with who found
the murdered woman's clothes

it was angie playing on
the jukebox on that last perfect day

couldn't remember ever growing
bored with being alive, but it's that chance
for greatness that always keeps
            passing us by

it's leonard's death that wakes me up on
some mornings, it's my father's on others

it's the suffocating weight of fear

the slower crush of passing days

wake up lost in the middle of
august and already
the air tastes like autumn

the shadows of clouds crawl across
the floor, across the fields and highways,
and what am i supposed to do with all
of the time we lost?

how much of your life
can you waste on regret?

and all of those pretty songs we
still keep trying to sing
through mouthfuls of dust and blood

John Sweet

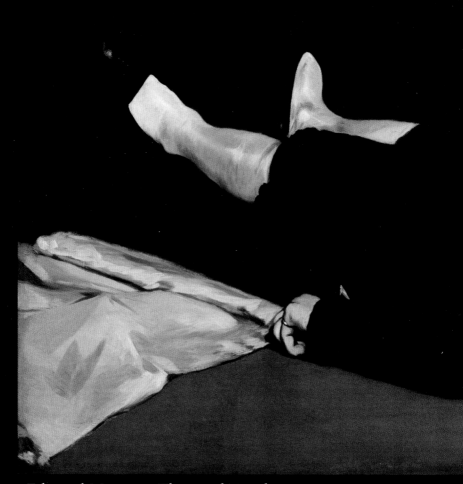

Edouard Manet — *The Dead Toredor*

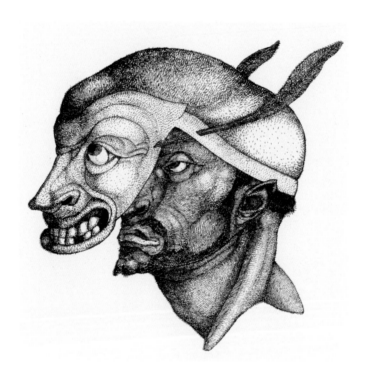

SpagDaddies

A Cautionary Tale

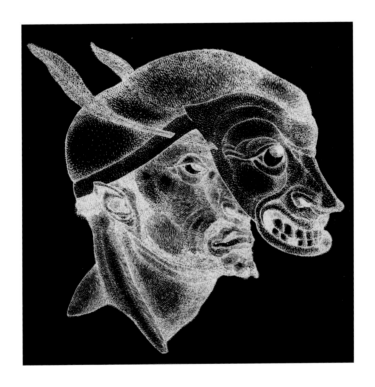

Leonard Baggs

They turned off the music and turfed us out. In our tens of thousands, we stumbled into the night. Starless. Cold. Sleep felt a million miles away but there was nothing else left. My grotty one-man tent seemed like the only option.

Then I heard a sound.

Something slow but funky. A strong baseline which carried across the field. I followed the music, tilting my head to try and locate its source. None of the people I passed seemed to notice. I rounded a corner and saw a large tepee. The sound grew — a guitar strut, bongo drums and soulful female vocals. People wandered, close by, oblivious. A sign beside the tent read Friendly Records. OPEN ALL NIGHT.

I stepped into 1974.

Moustaches, dungarees, large afros and buttoned-down shirts. Hairy chests, high-waisted trousers, platform shoes and perms. Big earrings. Bangles. A hive of shifting bodies, solo, pairs, groups, the floor moved as one. I bought a beer and stood by the side, wishing I could dance.

The entrance rustled and two figures entered. They had lank, greasy hair and they walked with stooped shoulders, their eyes cast down. One was dressed in a grubby trench coat, the other wore football shorts and wellies. They hugged the edge of the tent and moved around the dancers. A tall man in a black suit stood beside a velvet curtain. He nodded when the two figures approached, lifted the rope, and let them pass.

Strange.

I watched them disappear. They weren't staff — they wore neither the lanyards nor the wristbands. Was there another sound system back there? I finished my beer and threaded my way through the crowd.

'Can I come in?' I asked, flashing my staff wristband. The security guard did not move a muscle, his gaze resting beyond me. There was a strange smell — grilled cheese and unwashed genitals. Emblazoned on the lapel of the guard's jacket was a capital S, the top half yellow, the bottom red. I tried to sidestep and found a large hand pressed to my chest.

'Don't do this to yourself.'

He had a Russian accent. The other hand was balled up into a fist by his hip. Past his head I saw a mirrored wall with moving lights and shapes. I shrugged and turned around.

The dancers were in full swing. The DJ, a short man with a ponytail and high cheekbones, was mid-mix, his face inches from the spinning plates. The room vibrated with sexual charge. One of the dancers, a short woman with a silver leotard and fishnet stockings, caught my eye and beckoned with her finger. She was just my type, on the heavy side with thick hips and a rounded belly. Her thighs shook as she danced. She beckoned again, inviting me to take my place, to fold into the piles of oscillating flesh, but this was not my fate. I shook my head. Silver Leotard turned back to the crowd with a shrug. Time to leave.

The chip van was closed. Defeated, I trudged back to camp, the funny-shaped blue pill doing somersaults in my stomach and grinding the gears of my mind. The air was filled with the smell of compostable toilets. A group of lads emerged from the urinals, arm in arm, singing power ballads in many keys. I looked at the ground as I passed them by.

*

Anorak pillow and a pot to piss in. I gazed up at the canvas, taking the chewing gum on its thousandth journey around my gob as the wind flickered shadows and trembled zips. My mind turned to the woman in the silver leotard. The curl of her finger. What would it feel like to have her in my arms? To run my tongue along the soft folds of her belly.

I closed my eyes and tried to indulge the fantasy. Here. Beneath the torchlight. The way our bodies were designed to merge. But I am wretched. She shrinks at the rot of my teeth, at my sticky-fingered touch, at the rush of my animal shudder. I seed, two minutes at most, and the disappointment is hard to ignore. I offer affection, but the damage is done.

Even in dreams, I remained alone.

63

The tent collapsed with a rush of nylon. Pain. The bridge of my nose, my jaw, something in my belly. I could feel another body struggle against the flattened canvas. Violence stirred. I threw elbows, knees and short, sharp hooks, enjoying the thud of bone and flesh, the cries of pain from above me. Shouts became pleas of help. Amongst the scuffle flashed a bright orb of light. The orb struck my mouth and drew blood from my lips. I leant back and thrust up with both feet. The left connected and I felt my attacker stagger backwards, followed by a groan of pain.

I knelt up, supporting the broken tent with my hands as I tried to get my bearings. The orb was back, dancing around the side of the tent, followed by the sound of the zip.

'Sorry about all that pal. It's so bloody dark and I'm lugging this toolbox around. Although I must say, you put up quite a fight eh? Not that I blame you. I can tell this is an expensive make. Why don't you let me pay the damages? Fair is fair. Oh, where are my manners? Name's Alan.'

I blinked and reached up to shield my eyes. Alan was a short man with slicked back hair and a bushy moustache. He wore a blue boiler suit, unzipped several inches to reveal a hairy chest. In his right hand was a large toolbox, in the left a torch whose beam traced an outline around my crushed tent. I wiped away the blood which ran from my nose and my mouth. I wanted to hit him, but then I noticed the wound.

Several inches of tent pole emerged from a crimson stain on Alan's chest.

'Look, I'm in a bit of a rush,' said Alan, who seemed unaware of his injury. 'Duty calls. How about I come find you tomorrow and we can settle up?'

I watched him turn, pick up the toolbox, and totter off into the night, the pole protruding from his back. After several steps he collapsed to the floor.

'For fuck's sake.' I went over and helped Alan to his feet. He grabbed hold of my vest, a fistful of cloth, and staggered upright.

'Mind pulling this thing out of me lad? It's a bloody nuisance.'

Alan gestured to the tent pole. I took the torch from his hands and leaned in for a better look. The bloodstain now encompassed most of his torso. A punctured lung? Covered in my fingerprints? Alan looked pale. Emblazoned on his jumpsuit was a large S, the top half yellow, the bottom red.

'I'm going to take you to the medical tent.'

Alan sighed and checked his watch, an expensive looking silver thing which hung loosely off his wrist. He started off again, slipped, and fell against me.

'Alright then,' he said. 'If you wouldn't mind taking me toolbox? Ta.'

I leaned down to pick it up, but the box didn't budge.

'Put your back int'it,' said Alan by way of encouragement. I tried again, but the thing must've weighed at least fifty kilos. There was a handle at the end. I was able to raise one side and drag it behind me. We set off in a slow, wandering limp.

*

The festival was dead — nothing but the occasional vagabond and fields of litter. As we walked, Alan uttered an endless stream of meaningless chatter.

'Thing about them Rubicons — not the cans mind — those ones in cartons — mango, lychee — only certain shops —' he broke off in a fit off coughing — 'Problem with football — it's all about diet. Who cares what players eat broccoli? And another thing, don't get me wrong, I'm all for house plants, but some people go overboard. Like my auntie Rona — whole flat full of 'em. You can barely move in there.'

I tuned him out. The medical tent was by the main entrance and we had to cross the entire festival. I watched the world go past, the final creatures of the night; fuckboys in bucket hats, pupils like saucers, cougars in mixed-print on the lookout for young lovers, hasbeens with long beards and anoraks, looking shifty beneath the glow of electric lanterns.

'And they can barely shake their tails — crunchy not smooth — brought home a squeegee. Gamechanger.' he squeezed my shoulder. 'Lad, mind I make a quick stop? Then we can go get ourselves fixed up.'

Alan was very pale — half-lit by the torch clutched at his hip — waxen skin, blue-grey lips and bloodshot eyes. We were soaked in rain. He slipped out of my grasp. I looked up. Here we were. The Friendly Records Tent. Alan staggered inside and I followed after, dragging the toolbox behind me.

1974 had gone. In its place was 1929. A swing band. Couples in suits and short dresses danced the Charleston. It didn't even resemble a tent anymore. Chandeliers hung from the ceiling. Bartenders in waistcoats shook cocktails in time with the music. I reached up and touched a brickwork wall. Alan smiled and licked his lips.

'This way lad.'

I lugged the toolbox up a set of stairs and dragged it past a row of diners. A champagne cork whizzed past, followed by a roar of mirth. A group of men in tuxedos gathered around the bottle. It felt as though the toolbox had grown in weight — a crate of lead — and I had to turn and use two hands, craning my neck to face the direction of travel. Soon my back was wrecked. I stood up and found myself looking into a familiar face.

'A'rite Vitor,' said Alan, his head level with the big bouncer's chest. Vitor's face crumpled in concern.

'Alan, what has happened?'

'Never mind. My mate here's looking after me. I just need to make a quick stop. Booth seven's out of action. Probably needs a re-spool.'

Vitor nodded. 'Is he new?'

Alan turned to me and, using his thumbs, reached over and pulled down the skin beneath my eyes. They both leaned in to look.

'As a baby.'

Vitor smiled and patted me on the back.

'Welcome to church.'

We stepped through the velvet curtain and everything changed. Forever. I found myself in a narrow corridor whose walls, floor, and ceiling were covered with mirrors. Instantly disorientated I stumbled to the right, caught myself against the wall, and came face-to-face with my own reflection, bleeding from the nose and mouth, a cut along my brow, a bruise forming beneath my eye. I pressed my hand to the wall and mirror-me followed suit, fingertips touching, leaving behind little greasy smudges.

The corridor was filled with people — a rag-tag queue which we passed, pressed to the wall, apologising as the toolbox clattered against knees and shins. People were dressed in suits, pyjamas, kimonos, hippy pants, tracksuits, dashikis and martial arts uniforms, all gazing forwards with the same irreducible hunger in their sallow, yellowing eyes. At the end of the corridor stood a traffic light — the sort used for diversions and roadworks — set to red. I watched it turn yellow, then green, and an old man in a starched military uniform shuffled through. The queue moved forwards a pace, the light returned to red, and everyone stopped. Passing the crowd, we reached a set of turnstiles. Alan presented a fob to the machine, stumbled through, then passed the key back to me. Seconds later I got my first glimpse of SpagDaddies.

Filth. Magnificent filth. Thirteen booths, each no larger than a cash machine and separated by plywood boards. Each booth contained a figure on their knees, head buried in the depths of a primordial void. The air was filled with the sound of slurping.

Shluushshsslsusspsspuusshuussuslllusposohopup.

Slack jawed; hungry pulls; the air rent with strong cheese and body odour. I stood on the edge of the spectacle, caught between horror and awe. A few TVs dotted the cramped room. One showed golf, another cookery. The flatscreen beside me displayed go-pro-footage of a diver exploring a sunken wreck. Nobody watched.

'Cm'on lad. Don't be shy,' said Alan, waving me over. I followed, dragging the toolbox behind me as we made our way to booth number seven. Empty. Lit by a flashing red light.

'Just as I thought. Mind grabbing me a spanner?'

I opened the toolbox. It was filled with bricks. A couple of metal tools were stacked up to one side and a plastic bag was filled with monkey nuts. I removed a small adjustable spanner and passed it over.

'Ta.'

Alan unfastened a run of steel bolts, a mechanical sound against the backdrop of slurping mouths. I turned my attention to the booth.

In the centre was a protruding metal nub, like an underdeveloped water fountain, brown with rust and covered in dried matter. Beside the nub were two large buttons;

one yellow

the other red.

Alan unfastened the last bolt and removed a metal plate from the wall of the booth.

'Gimme a leg up lad.'

I offered Alan my hands, fingers interlaced. He hooked his foot in and, using me as a stirrup, guided himself into the hole. The tent pole brushed against the metal edge and Alan whistled with pain.

'You alright?'

'I really need that doctor. Thing is, Reverend Spag doesn't accept excuses. I have to get this bird working. Pass me through a screwdriver? Yeah, the Phillips one.'

I leaned over and passed the tool through the hole. Inside was a hive of motion. A steaming vat fed a series of mechanical arms which extruded blocks of mulch into a long, string-like substance.

'Is that … pasta?'

Alan didn't respond, my question lost in the whirr of machinery. The mechanism was vast and complicated, shrouded in darkness. Alan ducked under a pair of tubes which pumped red and yellow liquid and disappeared into the shadows. A few seconds later he reappeared, his face paler still. Droplets of blood had begun to collect in the corners of his eyes.

'Mind giving her a toot?' he asked. 'That's right, down on your knees like the rest of them. There's no special treatment here.'

I did as he asked. On my knees I was faced with the choice between the red and yellow buttons. I could no longer see his face.

'Which colour?'

'Up to you lad. It's all about preference.'

I chose yellow and made myself comfortable. The nub grew, swollen with feed, enlarging with a faint clicking sound. It was rusted and flecked with food. A cheesy, vomit-like odour emanated from it. Unsure of how, unsure of why, I wrapped my lips around the spout and began to suck.

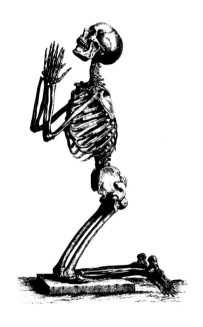

'Is it coming?' I heard Alan shout.

I do not respond, for I am far, far away. My first taste of SpagDaddies; a cord of wheat coated in a thick, cheesy sauce, the sort you buy in a packet at a cornershop, yet whose whole is more than the sum of its parts. It moves quickly, spooling up in my mouth, and I must chew, swallow, and suck all at the same time. Meanwhile, the flavour does something very special to my brain. It unlocks me. I have lived in a shallow pool yet, suddenly, I become aware of the ocean, of the soul, of my own fathomless depths. I experience the totality of things in a single moment.

Am I going to be sick?

No. It rises in my throat but, before I have a chance to heave, I am struck by a full-body orgasm. My knees shake, my jaw goes slack, and every cell vibrates as the soft starch of infinity pools out over my chest. Hot oil fills my beard and splashes against my skin.

This is the end

This is the beginning.

There is the time before, and then the age of SpagDaddies — a shallow existence — a continual lurch — from festival to layby to town hall to budget wedding celebration. We are storm chasers. We are Captain Ahab. We are bird watchers of the most twisted variety. I am SpagDaddies and SpagDaddies is me. How could it be any other way?

Time flares back into existence. Motion. The unchanging change. I look up, my mouth still shackled to the steel teat. Alan's demented face emerges from the hole. His eyes blaze and a sick smile plays out across his lips. He tries to pull himself out but, without me to help him, the exertion is too much and, finally, he dies — slumped forwards — half in half out.

Perhaps I will take his place. Sure, the overalls will be a little small, but I can make it work. A few weeks to get to grips with the machinery. Learn the ropes. It isn't as if anyone will miss me.

Werner Galow

Werner Galow is an artist from Cologne. His work is inspired by comics, movies, news and books.

Werner Galow — *The Secret of the Shoemaker*

Werner Galow — *Just a Little Nightmare*

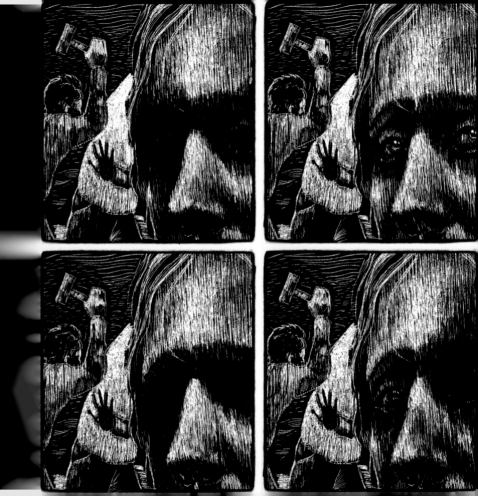

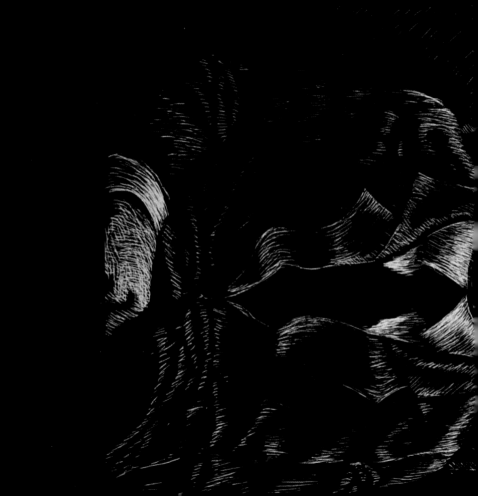

Timber knows nothing

To exist
(or to be alive),
we certainly lead a lifestyle ...

to hit the mark
(being correct and successful),
there are a small number of us

帶 渴 動 群 過 的 一 一 生 在
有 被 長 隨 他 空 無 些 活 手
異 蓋 腿 意 們 缺 所 我 中 仍
物 住 口 走 牛 通 知 們 有 的

(perhaps surprising or unexpectedly)
with no home or means.

To know, understand and comprehend
the aim, standard and criterion
(the optimal potential in each emerging moment)
is inadequate.

Through them,
awesome and powerful
(maybe even stubborn, pig-headed and arrogant)
multitudes
follow, heed and accompany ...
wishing and intending
to journey
growing, developing, nourishing and honouring
the foundation named 'thirsty and tired.'

Scattering nonsense, bragging and deception
is a dwelling where existence is —
metaphorically —
death.

Freedoms and privileges
exist
in real life ...
not fiction.

Ours is nothing
to know or understand
through them —
a group of people
lost
(or wandering from the truth)
contrary to their choice, desire, disposition, purpose or
import.

The shank — whether prolonged, distant or vast —
is thirsting to be enveloped
with external
wealth, deeds and topics.

Timber knows nothing.

Freedom, love or fondness
in life is ours.

In what is right, fitting and direct —
that is the 'herd' to be or remain always ...
wandering or wavering in
will, joy or delight
is wearisome
(a foot thirsty to hide from the outside curdles itself
fatalistically).

Douglas Colston

Who? The 'Sin-see'

這 新 哪 哪
新 詞 個 個
詞 詞 個 新
詞 新 詞 詞
新 個 新 不
這 詞 這

Everywhere,
a single 'Sin-see'
makes afresh
words, excuses, apologies, shirking, refusal,
resignation, dismissal and contrarianism.

A 'Sin-see'
is a prattling contrarian …
a thing
like an indefinite determiner   नव्य शप् क सा
or a rhetorical question.

Welcoming, greeting or receiving
a 'Sin-see'
is the death of change or reform.

Immediately change that!

A new oath: ΩΘΕΩ·ΕΙΣ·ΝΕΑ·ΛΕΘ·
happiness, joy and pleasure
giving, granting and bestowing.

86

Pushing unity —
youthful, fresh, unexpected, strange or (potentially) evil
speech or words …
like novel, infantile, new, unusual, strange or
extraordinary
words, proverbs or discourse.

If only refreshment, reinvigoration and reform
were guaranteed
(only 'new' is assured).

'Sin-see' —   ᛒᚠᚱᚠ·ᛏᛅᛏᛏ·ᛟᚱᚦ·
by the way —
is a homonym
of the Chinese term
for 'neologism' …
now that
is neat!

Douglas Colston

John Singer Sargent — *Man Wearing Laurels*

John Singer Sargent — *Padre Sebastiano*

CONQUERQUISTADOR

Veni, Vidi, Vici proclaimed the greatest conqueror.
Prophetically cyclical that
eternal return.
Ouroboros it was, is, ever will be.

They came
through splendorous virgin seas,
guided under a faithful star
westward for glory and wealth.
Distance unknown hearts set,
three argosies consigned.
The first Cynic cackled.

They saw
bountiful raw shores and bore
gifts of gold, spice, myrrh.
Slivery tongues spouted slithering lies
lustful candor in their eyes
beguiled Astraea.
The pale star faded, in shade the sacred tear fell.

They plundered
under the red sun, bodies scattered
bathed in the salty scent of bloody Neptune's
accursed shores under charcoal skies.

Cannons the voice of gods
sundered the halcyon spring.
Tenochtitlan to ash.

Ruined cities sit still, now broken
deadlands, concrete valleys.
Monuments once mighty now fallen, crumbled
nesting places for birds.
This is how our world ends —
with a whimper,
after the bang.

Ryan J.M. Tan

First, you worshipped the wrong God.
Man was not omniscient, He
could not save you.
You ignored the Goddess who had all the answers.
Then, you realised She could solve the crisis
so you called to Her, begged Her for forgiveness.
But Mother Nature didn't respond
you already destroyed Her in your ignorance.

Now, you wish upon the moon,
because the moonlight can still
penetrate the orange clouds.
The stars are long gone.

Chloe Utting

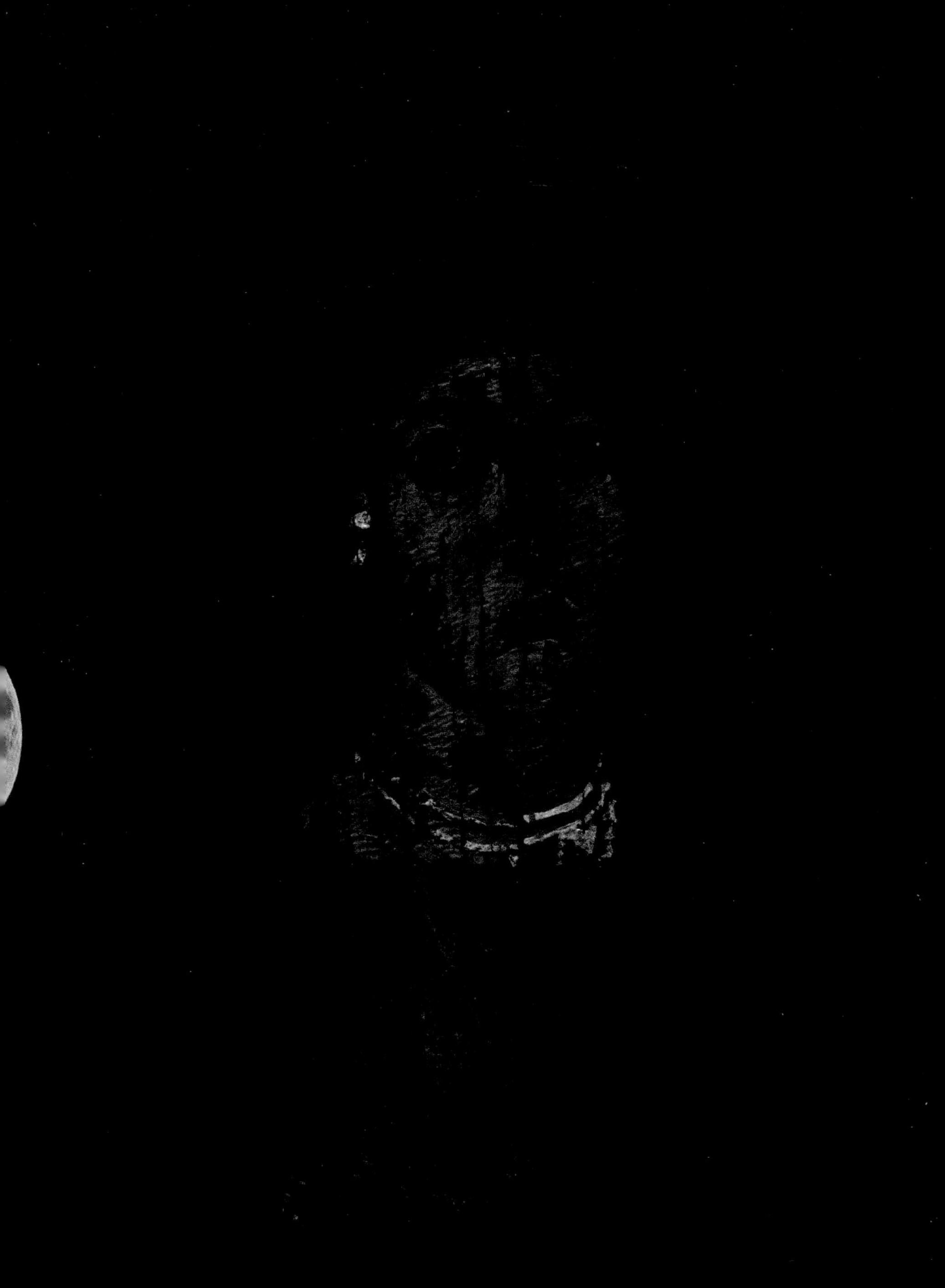

Eduard Tolos Palau

Kabba the Invisible Rainbow

Eduard Tolos Palau — *Darkness Move No 5*

I remember walking through the forest and feeling the dead trees call me. They still had life, something rare, something that pushed me to carve into the soil and dig up the root. The heart. I had a feeling there was something inside the wood, something that commanded me to carve, cut, and polish it, bringing the tree heart back to life.

Since then, every time I find a tree heart, the work comes to me, out of nowhere. My sculptures contain trapped souls trying to escape our world. People warned me that these figures were the whispers of spirits, that I was materialising demons, bringing them back to the material plane, that I should stop, but ... I can't. Kabba the Invisible Rainbow informs me of things outside our perception, things which exist yet cannot be seen. When we discover them, we have the power to change everything.

Eduard Tolos Palau — *Darkr*

love No 2

Eduard Tolos Palau — *Darkness Move No 4*

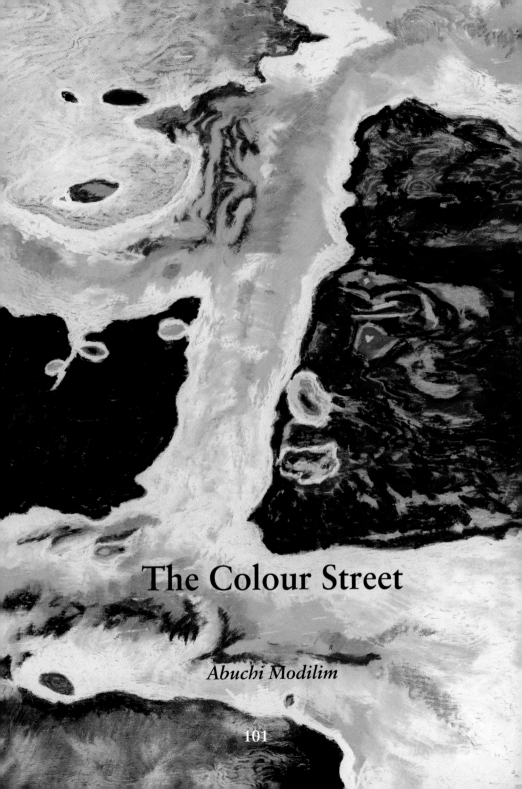

The Colour Street

Abuchi Modilim

Mad people lived here. Sad people lived here. Evil people lived here. God left this place before we were born.

102

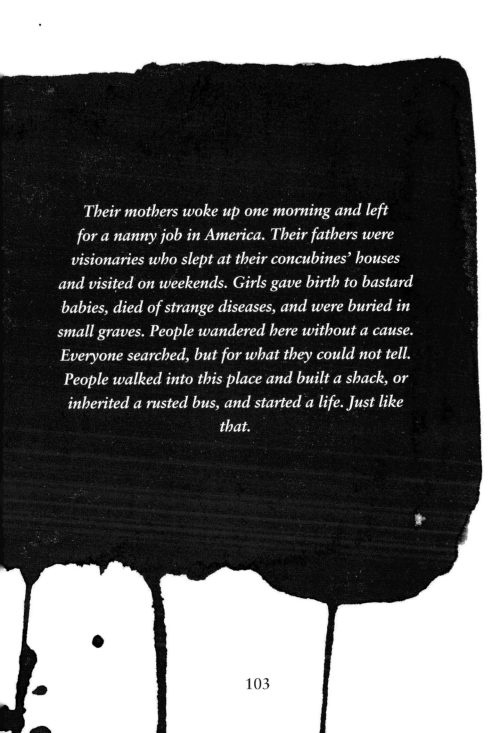

*Their mothers woke up one morning and left
for a nanny job in America. Their fathers were
visionaries who slept at their concubines' houses
and visited on weekends. Girls gave birth to bastard
babies, died of strange diseases, and were buried in
small graves. People wandered here without a cause.
Everyone searched, but for what they could not tell.
People walked into this place and built a shack, or
inherited a rusted bus, and started a life. Just like
that.*

A short man on tiny-tiny dada walked into the neighbourhood, a Ghana-must-go hanging from his right shoulder, and moved into the rusting bus where we hid, kissed, and touched the girls who played our wives. We named him Sangolo. The mothers thrust their heads through the windows of their shacks and whispered.

'That man is mad. Onye ala, why hasn't he come to greet our husbands?'

'I think he will not stay for a long time. Mosquitoes will finish him.'

'Every madman come here when they leave their chain.'

'One day, children sellers will come as madmen and carry our children. We must not remove our eyes from that man.'

The fathers did not mention Sangolo at their gathering. They did not care about anyone who would not give them money or pay for their drinks. They discussed football and laughed into the quietness of the evening.

The next morning we woke to the usual noises — shouts of the bus conductors, whistles of the vigilante men, the dogs barking. The door of the bus had been painted red and blue, sprinkled with yellow. Sangolo whistled while he mixed colours in a wooden bowl. A small crowd gathered. We had not seen this kind of painting before. We were used to the paintings artists sell in traffic; portraits of Fela, Lucky Dube, Bob Marley and Nelson Mandela.

'It is the validity of Thought, the magic of Vincent Van Gogh. Perception of painting is universal. Everything we cannot fathom,' said Sangolo without looking up.

The mothers whispered.

'He is talking like one who knows book.'

'What is this thing he drew? It is like what my son can draw.'

'He is showing his madness in painting.'

'This man is possessed. The Devil is using him.'

The fathers went down the road to Mama Fullstop's kiosk, where they drink and play draught. It was their duty to drink at Mama Fullstop's every morning. Girls came with their phones and took pictures of the painting. One girl, Diamond, recorded a video to post on Facebook.

When everyone had left my father walked to the bus and stood with his hands folded, watching the painting. He had stopped laughing after God took my mother on

Christmas day of last year. That night, after my mother was laid in a small grave at the back of our shack, Pastor Thunder told my father that it was God, not cancer, that took my mother. It was from my mother that I learned that God was a woman. She called her ala na azu nwa during morning prayers. My father never forgave God for taking my mother. He stopped giving me books to read and having long conversations with me.

We knew that, since Sangolo had occupied our bus, the games would be limited. We could not play the Husband-and-Wife game, and we could not touch the girls and have them touch us. We were five friends. Nono was the son of a lonely ashawo. The men climbed his mother then deserted her when she gave birth to Nono. Pastor Thunder said we were created in the image and likeness of God, but Nono resembled every man in the neighbourhood. Chinne was the daughter of a widow who entertained men when the sky was dead. Nnenne, whose mother had married a new man, told us her stepfather used his tongue and long fingers on her body, and Bobo was the son of a drunkard who beat his mother and spread her legs to the sun.

'Let us carry his paint and run away,' Nono suggested.

'My mother said he is mad. He will bite us,' Nnenne replied.

'Forget that thing. We will carry his paint and nothing will happen,' said Bobo, leading the way.

The painting now covered the entire side of the bus. Sangolo had sprinkled it with brown and green. He smiled at us while we conversed in whispers.

'This man will bite anyone who nears his paint. He is smiling like English, the mad man,' said Chinne.

'Chinne is right, let us leave,' said Nnenne.

That evening me and my father ate thick egusi soup. I thought of my mother every time I dipped the akpu in the egusi. For once, my father did not listen to the 9 pm news or play the songs of Celestine Ukwu.

'Too-boy, watch over the house. I will be back soon.'

He picked up my mother's rubber food flask and took the road towards the bus.

*

The bus was rough and dirty, flecked with white. We could not tell what Sangolo was painting. He walked the length of the bus, sprinkling it with different colours. Fathers joined the iPhone girls. Mothers whispered.

'Who said that this man is not a craze somebody?'

'He will draw on our shacks after drawing on this bus.'

'I thought that book was the expression for these madmen. I never knew they express their madness in painting.'

The girls took pictures, arguing whose camera was brighter while Sangolo lay down and looked up at the bus's rusting roof.

My father stood there with his hands on his waist. When my mother was alive I used to imagine that he had a pinch of sky in his eyes. His eyes smiled when his face was quiet. When everyone had left my father entered the bus and sat near Sangolo, who got up and began mixing colours. The mothers whispered from their makeshift kitchens.

'What is Ben doing with a mad man inside the bus, onye ala?'

'Ben I see now is not the Ben I see when the wife was living. That woman carried him like a child.'

'Madmen know themselves everywhere.'

My father took a pot of jollof rice off the fire and told me to serve myself when I was ready to eat. I imagined him talking to Sangolo.

I was a journalist in the sixties. If I told you that I travelled to America would you believe? I will never forget those beautiful days when life was good. I published articles that the government found threatening. Who doesn't know Ben Ikeorah? I ran here, to this secluded place, thinking I would find my way out of the country, but they confiscated everything. Nna'm, man had to move on. I work with a bread factory now that pays my salaries in half. Imagine. I have seen and touched money. At the end of the day what is important is that we heal.

By the time Sangolo sprinkled another colour on the painting, the smile in my father's eyes would broaden.

113

Sangolo left the neighbourhood and my father took ownership of the bus. Mothers whispered on the road and in the corners of shacks.

'Madness finally hit Ben.'

'Does he want to move into the bus?'

'We have to help him before it's too late.'

My father ignored them and spent his evenings in the bus after work, reading newspapers and playing the songs of Celestine Ukwu. We dared not enter the bus to play.

A week later we heard on the news. A museum in the US was looking for the man who painted a bus in a Nigerian ghetto. They offered a ten thousand dollar reward. That evening everyone danced, sang, and praised God. The grownup boys left to find Sangolo. The iPhone girls had taken pictures of the painting that had gone viral on Facebook. Everyone with money bought the newspaper, with its pictures of our neighbourhood and its caption — THE COLOUR STREET.

'See, is this not my shack on the newspaper?'

'This is the back of my head. My wealth will come from this place.'

'I knew that man was a messenger of God, here to carry us up.'

'The government will give our area attention now.'

This time, gathering to watch the painting which brought them fame, they paid close attention.

'I think this is a man walking into a dark place.'

'This is shadow that I am seeing.'

'Look from this side, it is a woman.'

'It is a big head, bend like this.'

What I saw was a dirty painting screaming freedom.

Oyibos from different museums in America came in big cars and said they wanted to buy the painting. It was our first time seeing oyibo people in real life. My father, being the most intelligent man in the neighbourhood and owner of the bus, spoke with them. Everyone had forgotten the madness that hit my father. They led him into the corner of a shack and whispered.

'Ben, do not let them deceive you. You know book. Show them you know book.'

'How much are they pricing the bus? Tell them it is fifty thousand naira.'

'Please tell them I am available in case any of them want boyi boyi.'

'Tell them about my son. He can paint that thing.'

'If it is ten thousand they are paying then let them pay. I have not drank anything today.'

My father nodded at their requests.

The museum representatives bid for the painting; ten thousand dollars, fifteen thousand dollars, twenty-five thousand dollars. A woman with long hair, nose, face and legs bid forty-five thousand dollars and everyone fell quiet. Nobody believed her until she came back with a tipper that would carry the bus, handing a leather bag full of dollars to my father. The money was shared out among the families of the neighbourhood. We sang and danced all the dances we knew. Mineral drinks were bought for children and mothers at Mama Fullstop's. The fathers drank beer. The iPhone girls announced we were trending on Twitter. Everyone was awake until the next morning. That night God had left the moon reaching for our laughter. It was her way of sharing in our joy, since she couldn't come down to this dirty place anymore.

The next morning vendors came into our neigbourhood baby-carrying newspapers with different headlines; THE GRACE GHETTO, THE GRASS TO GRACE SLUM and GOD REMEMBERS A SLUM. I hated this last headline. Which God? The God who took no pity on our suffering? Many fathers went to change dollars at the bank and never returned. Their wives spoke to the bastard grownup boys.

'I know my husband is still changing dollars. He will buy me High Wax when he comes back.'

'When my husband comes back, we will leave here, go to the city, and live in a big house.'

'It is evil people that are whispering to the bank not to change my husband dollar.'

'We have suffered together. He is on the road coming back. I saw it in my dream.'

They ran out of their shacks whenever a car passed through the neighbourhood. Then they got disappointed, smiled the 'it is well' smile, and began to mould hope afresh; a liquid thing, envious of their faith. To this day they believe their husbands are at the bank, changing dollars.

My father paid strong boys to dig up my mother's bones. They took her to the burial ground and laid her to rest. My father came back in a yellow taxi, asked me to wear my fine clothes, and told me we were leaving for Lagos. The driver arranged our Ghana-must-gos in the boot and the neighbouring shacks came to say goodbye. The women whose husbands were still changing dollars thanked my father, praising him for lifting them when they were just beginning to hug suffering. I watched from the back seat as the car galloped from the neighbourhood. I watched my friends in the rear mirror, running after the taxi and waving at me as their laughter changed to small cries; the type of cry that makes you catch your breath, scoop hot air from your heart and leave it to boil in your throat. The type of cry I cried when my mother died. This God, who claimed to be faithful, had abandoned my friends too, and their mothers — her fellow women. Bobo's father and Nnenne's stepfather lived at the bank now. The bastard grownup boys visited their mothers late at night. Wives don't leave their husbands. The wives who left in the past were cursed. Women have to die with pain shouting on their bodies so they can rise with Christ on the last day. Pastor Thunder poured salt water on their dead bodies and left. Nobody knew if he was going to the bank, or to heaven, and the women were buried without consolation. No prayers to rest their spirits, no salt water to holy their bones, just dead bodies in homemade caskets, embracing the earth that compressed their bodies.

We moved into a furnished room with a toilet in Lagos. My father made arrangements for us to leave for America. I heard on the news that the museum looking for Sangolo had increased the prize money to twenty thousand dollars. Every night in my dream, I saw Sangolo painting our bus with different colours and, every morning, I woke up before I could ask him where he'd gone.

Second Nature

creepy, hairy, weird guy
can't fly and doesn't want to
eat from human hand
loves to devour ketchup
on motherfucking meatloaf
and burp the bloody alphabet

you can't take more than two steps
on any path, or you trigger
a transformation, something worse
than this guy with shotgun laughter
cracking fleas between his teeth
and pissing in the alley

he's always in transition
we whisper out of range
kenneled in foster homes, halfway houses
raised a feral child, he can't help his nature
his suspect morals, lunatic temper

sometimes I catch him outside the local den
drawing in the scent of pine, clearing his head
staring at the bald-faced moon
scratching behind his ear

he talks about his unformed dreams
a need to travel, do something
it almost seems at that moment
he comes across as normal

Colleen Anderson

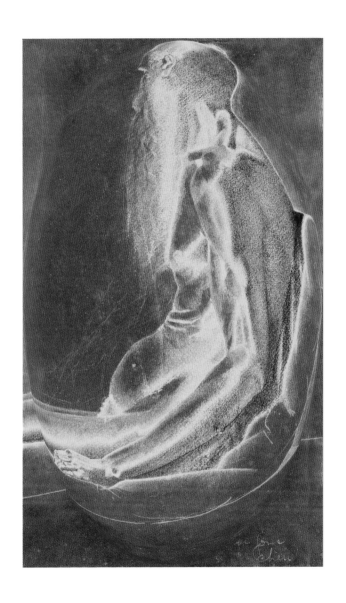

Sycamore

I can close my eyes &
count the hidden boughs...

Nessa raised them all
in the metal earth
b'fore wading into sunset.

The true trees are ones
with no shade;
to remind body
there's no home,
like place of rest
when midriff still
remembers the contraction
of cramps & tussle of hips.

For the magic
of dead eyes;
how wrong it was
to think,
It is clever to
throw our sick friends
into the night,
out of weariness,
into a miraculous cloud
we have not touched.

This breed. Exotic.
women washed their babies,
sanctified their spirits &
put them to sleep on
the latex leaves.
Like sky, green, broad...
it is the sea —
watching the fisherman
drown in expectation,
behind the howling torrent.

What is known to me
is the pale truth;
the uncertainty of water,
how despite its chaos
I find stillness
reclining on a fin.

How hard it is
to disbelieve,
night & day is insect —
is firefly.
is a fantasy I'll record
on the barn door.
Until dusk
every revelation
is a prodigy.

Gabriel Awuah Mainoo

Art, love & onions

for Lina

I believe there is war
in every making — not in the doing alone

however in the thinking &
at arrival; the final touch
of your magical artifact

how sweet an imperfect poem blooms
on a galley proof, not for the rhyming
but how even with errors

the poet's imperfect life is
beautiful & neatly tacked into a book
& not knowing its origin on the shelf

amidst the unlabeled pile of books you
bring it down & place it under the holy books.

The only cure to war;
do not name the thing one.
you carve a synonym from life
and call it art.

The cinders of the years
gather at your feet; Lina
in every corner of the kitchen lurks
the malice, that chokes you sweetly

you feel the gnaw of
fire, smoke the sharp cut of
a tomato tin
& the strong scent of a rotting onion.

The rising odor of onion
is grief
you keep it at a distance where
its cruelty does not lance the pupil.

You cannot shield the
eyes from what it does not see.

The way to end a thing
begins with
drowning it at the base

So you tie a bandana, &
slice your onion wafer-thin under water.

The early April rains;
the freshness of our blooming,
the over-floating hollow

behind the tennis court,
above the cleanliness,
mirrors clandestine desires of you
yellow, me, blue, me, finding you

you, finding me
in the rushing & floating & bubbling of raindrops.

Gabriel Awuah Mainoo

Love is the Thing
With
Teeth

Philip Webb Gregg

Says Mr Wolf

His eyes are not yellow like beeswax but grey like a road. He sits anxious in the chair, limbs wrapped in prison clothes, brow glistening. I had expected something else. Confidence and charm. Oozing lust. Some smooth and dangerous figure with a tongue to match. I had not expected this.

It's something of an anti-climax, after all that I've heard.
All the witness statements, the files and the photos. All
of the stories. I'd have thought he'd tread blood into the
carpet and splinter the mirror as he passed.

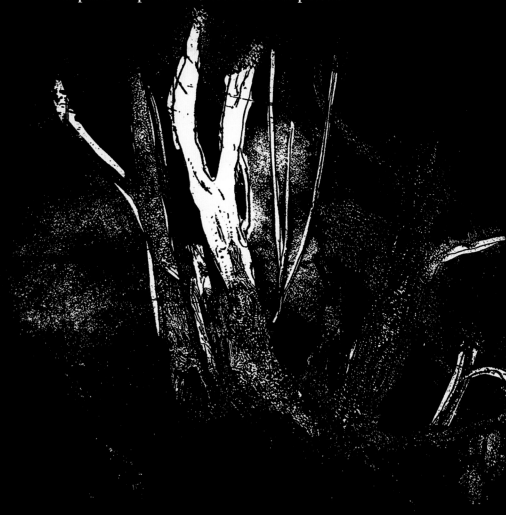

But no. Instead he babbles. Words crowding together like
rodents leaping a forest fire. It's quite sad, really.

His beard is thin. It stretches unevenly across his face and neck. A bad case of acne blotches his left cheek. Some of the spots are open wounds and the white pus gleams like pearls amid the red ruined earth of his face.

Occasionally he runs his hands over his hair in a nervous gesture, and the sweat from his palms smears wetly on his otherwise dry curls, spoiling the last possibility of good looks.

In the months leading up to this meeting there have been dozens of security checks. His jailers have told me — in no uncertain terms — what kind of man he is. What kind of creature. They said that I should be careful. No, it was more than that: they say I should be afraid.

Said he was triggered by women, and that it would be wise if I wore plain, unrevealing clothing. Ideally black.

They said nothing with a hood, and especially nothing red. Not even a sock. They were very particular about this.

Not even a single red sock, they said.

regret it as soon as it escapes his lungs. I wonder if I should add Schizoaffective to my list.

All of them. I've read every one, since forever. I promise you. I have.

I ask him to clarify. Surely, I say, he doesn't expect me to believe that he has read every work of literature since the dawn of civilization?

Oh, God no! Long before that.

He gives me a serious look and then lets out another burst of awkward laugher. I cross my arms, getting uninterested fast. Ask him how is that possible? What does he mean by that? But he merely hums and fidgets. After a few minutes of skittish silence, in which I scrawl *Psychomotor Agitation*, he suddenly looks up. His gaze vacant. Hollow and sharp, his grey eyes bite into mine.

It's easy, you see. They all belong to me. A smile, and for the slightest instant there is something vile and handsome in his features. *They all know it, really. They know it in the red-wet-dark of their hearts. All the words are mine. I'm Mr Wolf, you know. And every love story is a blood story.*

The interview continues in a similar way. Back and forward we play the game. He gives obscure speeches and taps his feet with awkward laughter, criss-crossed by the occasional bout of vacant silence.

The whole thing begins to feel circular. I'm wasting my time. This isn't cat and mouse, it's a mutt chasing its own tail.

After an hour he asks if he can go to the bathroom. I sigh, say that he can. I knock for the guards and together they tread their ugly boots down the prison hallway. When he's gone, I rap the pen thoughtfully against my front two teeth. I'm aware that something is wrong.

Not for the first time I ask myself what I'm doing here. What do I want from this? What, after all, do I have to learn from Mr Wolf? Given the things I already know. The death, the murder, and worse. The shadow that circles him like a second sun. Why do I think this meeting will make a difference?

And then — from nowhere — it comes to me, and I bite
down on the tip of my pen.

With my mouth full of ink I say it out loud,
spluttering dark blotches on my blouse
(a plain grey one, as advised).
I laugh with the absurdity of it.

The stark every-day-ness of my epiphany.
It's the equivalent of witnessing a miracle
mid-way down a shopping isle.

A metaphor spoken from a blood-hungry mouth.

When he returns there is red on his face. I'm shocked for a moment and then I realize it's the spots. He's been squeezing them.

His hair looks different too. He's smoothed it down and slicked it back. He stands straighter, and am I imagining things, or has the colour of his eyes changed?

You have more questions, Doc?

He says, sitting down and tapping the arm of the chair with his fingers

I notice his nails.

Every single one has been chewed to a stub.

I look at him for a while and then shake my head.

Turn the page on my notebook.

No more questions.

Just tell me a story.

Bomb Threat

We are afraid of telling people our names.
We are afraid to wear scarfs in public, of knowing the
moment we do they'll stare, follow us around in suspicion
and
spit where we walk. Rocks following their swears.

We are afraid of losing luggage in an airport: police in
masses
trying to defuse what is actually our razor. We are afraid
of the
anal checks and x-rays after showing them our
beards under our masks; praying to God that we didn't
shove a bomb up our
ass in our sleep.

We are afraid of university accommodation, surrounded
by
'people' who've never seen someone placing their face to
the floor
five times a day.
We are afraid that nothing will ever change.
We are afraid, so very afraid, that we'll misplace ourselves
to truly belong.

Naadia A. Hussein

Handyman

Nice old fellow
on his own
soft voice
big hands
slow feet
not bothered
by children or dogs
studies the damage
makes eye contact
can't be trusted
on account of
his rotten ladder.

Philip Davison

Counting the Ways

I am a creature of moments,
of wake ups and appointments and messages.
I am a native of intervals,
of meetings and sleeps and jobs
I am a captive of aging,
of sickness and slowness and stupor.

But in deliberate, amorphous chunks
I have been able to shrug off time.
Woods treks of no serious purpose,
fly fishing to the rhythm of the casts,
running long and unmeasured,
my mind free-swimming in eternity.
There is magic in motion.

Ed Ahern

Isabel Álvarez

In Conversation with Jack Jenkins

I first met Isabel Álvarez during university, nearly ten years ago. She was thirty-four, Spanish, shy yet articulate, arriving at each session well-prepared and happy — in contrast to her class-mates (myself included), who would turn up confused and hungover. Me and Isabel took the same bus to university and, gradually, became friends. It wasn't until the final seminar that I learned she liked to paint.

It's a bit of a cliché, but Álvarez paints like nobody's watching. She imagines no viewer, no critic, no customer. For her, it is the magic of mark-making and the simple joy of colour. She has been painting for twenty-five years and never sought an audience. In fact, until the publication of this book, less than a dozen people have seen her work. The result is a raw, unconscious style — populated by faces, moving bodies and a kind of jumbled, fluid geometricism. Her paintings come out of her like a fever dream; a revelation; a forgotten secret. When she paints, there is nowhere to hide.

Isabel Álvarez — *Self Portrait*

It is April and I am in London for a gig. I text Isabel, looking for somewhere to crash, and she tells me there is a spare sofa at her place in North London. I pop over mid afternoon. It is the first time I have been to her house. She leads me down an alleyway and into a narrow garden. There are paintings everywhere, half covered in vines and bushes, in various stages of completion. There is something sinister, almost violent, about the way her style combines with the run down garden. They lie in wait, sunk in mud, hidden behind bikes and paint-pots and rusted spades, lingering like shabby, punkish Picassos. We drink coffee and I tell Isabel about Goatshed Press. She seems interested but, when I ask her if she might feature, she says an emphtatic no. Isabel was in a crash as a child and suffered severe burns to her face and neck. In person she appears confident, unbothered by the exposed scars, but it has left her with an aversion to publicity, a tendency to keep her head down and avoid photographs. We chat some more, finish our coffee, then I leave for the gig. Weeks later, in the middle of the night, Isabel messages me to say she has changed her mind. I ask her if we might do an interview, something to accompany the paintings and, instantly, she agrees. We meet again in July. I drag the paintings from their positions in the garden, photograph them, then stack them up along the fence. Our interview happens at dusk with a bottle of wine and a bowl of crisps. Behind her stands her work, stretched along the fence like a silent, unblinking audience.

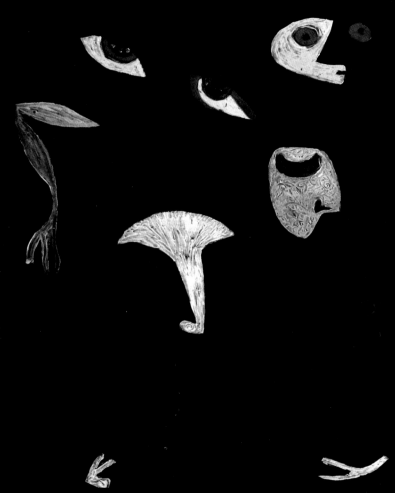

Isabel Álvarez — *Forest Feelings*

1ore in line with ordinary life?

Z: (laughs) You are really taking on the role of
ectual interviewer aren't you? I hope you don't
o much from my answers. No. I don't do things
r that reason. I paint on them because they are
  front of me. Do you know how expensive a
?

IEWER: But aren't you concerned that the
  will rip over time, the edges will fray, the wood
vaterlogged?

Z: Do you want to know a secret? Every year
ut down the back seat of my car, fill it up with
then take them all to the tip. That is my 'artistic
— I paint on trash, then throw it away.

IEWER: That makes me sad. Think of all the
ho could've been moved, transported by your

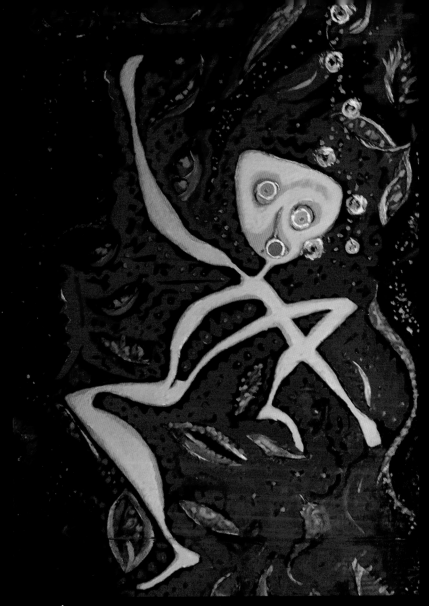

Isabel Álvarez — *Lime Cordial*

INTERVIEWER: What is your first memory of painting?

ÁLVAREZ: I remember stealing a tray of pastels from school and drawing landscapes when everyone went to bed. Where I'm from, the scenery is brutal. It hangs there like a thing you cannot forget. I remember hiding these drawings from my father, stuffing them beneath the mattress. He would have beaten me if he had found them. He was not a nice man.

INTERVIEWER: These days, all of your paintings contain the human form, there are bodies, hands, faces. Why does this subject, more than anything else, dominate your work?

ÁLVAREZ: Why ... why, always why. You are like the shrink who tries to intepret everyone's dreams. You do not get closer to the truth by analysing it. The thing, the painting, the dream, is the best way of articulating something, some secret the universe is trying to tell you. To explain is to miss the point.

INTERVIEWER: I see what you mean, but this is an interview ...

(we both laugh)

ÁLVAREZ: True true. I am sorry, I'm not very good at this. Go on, ask another question. I will try and give you something to write in your magazine.

ep these days. I've never shown anyone my paintings
cause I see no purpose in it. The joy is in slapping
lour on cardboard. Once it is finished the painting is a
ad thing. Who cares what other people think. But then,
hought, Jack is my friend. He is starting his magazine.
ese are hard times for everybody. We must not build
alls around our lives.

INTERVIEWER: Say the unimaginable happens. Say we
ublish this edition, it is a runaway success, and you are
e star of the book. Say, suddenly, auction houses are
amouring to buy your paintings, outbidding each other
crazy sums. What then? Would you still be able to
ake up, go down to your shed, and paint the first thing
at comes to your mind?

VAREZ: No. At least, I don't think so. It's what happens
en I try to write. Before I commit a single word to paper
ave imagined an audience, even if it's just a lover or

of gimmick, but as a living,

hing. Do you have any thoughts

a painter and a lover of stories?

(Pauses for a moment, watching

which holds the cigarette) When

to express yourself in a certain

e always going to rub up against

its. Take movies, for example.

the movie is an image — a kind

painting — but, you also get

words spoken by the characters.

ve no way of getting inside the

heads — there is the voiceover

INTERVIEWER: So, how do the limits of visual art and litetature differ? How might they interact with one another?

ÁLVAREZ: Fiction can only succeed by going beyond itself — by bringing us to something behind language.

INTERVIEWER: How do you mean?

ÁLVAREZ: Think about it. Nobody cares about little shapes on a piece of paper. Nobody weeps because these things are arranged just so. They cry and laugh because they have been taken to a place inside themselves. Somewhere they have lost or perhaps they never knew they had. That, to me, seems like the challenge of stories. How to, for a moment, let the reader forget that they are looking at squiggles on a block of pulped up tree. How to remind them of who they really are. Or who they might be. Painting doesn't have this problem. It sits beneath these things. In painting there is no logic. No intepretation. It is a dream — or a nightmare. It shows us directly how things are

...ations of painting.

AREZ: It is frozen, of course. A
[boo]k unfolds through time. A book
[is] to say — here is how things are,
[and] this happens, and look. Look
[how] life changes us. Look what can
[happ]en when we least expect it. A
[pain]ting is a single thing. It is the
[blink] of an eye. Great paintings seem
[to c]hange, seem to be alive, but they
[can] never tell the story of a life. See!
[You] have tricked me into talking like
[an i]ntellectual, ha! But, I suppose
[th]is what you mean when you talk
[abou]t putting the two things side by
[side.] Words can stretch a painting
[out.] Words can make a painting
[mov]e, can give it the shape and flow
[of a] story. Paintings — well I guess

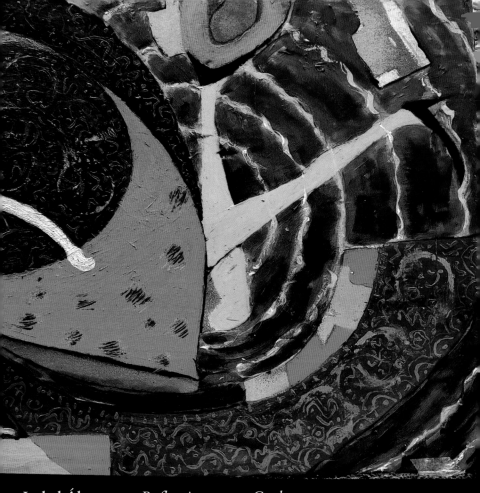

Isabel Álvarez — *Reflections on a Cyclone*

ÁLVAREZ: Can I ask you a question?

INTERVIEWER: Sure.

ÁLVAREZ: You're going show my paintings, and make them available for people to buy prints, right?

INTERVIEWER: Only if you want me too.

ÁLVAREZ: No. That isn't my point. What I'm saying is, if you sell them, then they need to be listed. To do that, don't the paintings need a name?

INTERVIEWER: Yeah, you better think of something to call them.

ÁLVAREZ: Let's do it now. Together.

And that is how the evening ends, in the shabby garden beside the shed, on our fourth glass of wine as the sun dips down behind the row of terraced houses. We take in turns to walk up to a painting, study it for a moment, then call it the first name which comes to mind.

Isabel Álvarez — *Me; A Boy*

nd originals of Álvarez's work are
Goatshed Press. For more informati
artclub@gmail.com

168

RE: YOUR CHIROPTEROLOGY VISA

Mirri Glasson-Darling

Dear Applicant,

We, The Review Board for XXO9 visa applications of Country 1, regret to inform you that we have rejected your application for the Chiropterologist Exemption 5A and summarily the XXO9 visa — allowing citizens of alien countries an opportunity to seek employment, academic study, and fall in love with our own citizens. We do this, having already received the corresponding paperwork and request from Citizen A of Country 1. The evidence submitted of your romantic bond over correspondence throughout the last four years was compelling, but there are other requirements the application did not meet. Precisely, it was the satisfaction of condition 2.xx of the Chiropterologist Exemption 5A that was deemed insufficient.

We appreciate that, knowing that our country has a shortage in chiropterologists, you outlined your chiropterology research plan in the study of bats. While of great interest to us, this alone was not enough to push your application through as 2.xx relates to other personal factors. Your work regarding the glycoprotein draculin as found in the saliva of desmodous rotundus or the 'Common Vampire Bat' is something we found particularly interesting. We were able to see the practical application of your research on the vampire bats projected migratory patterns in Country 1 as global temperatures rise: a topic of some national concern. We are already experiencing a troubling population increase in local populations of desmodous rotundus around the globe and Country 1 in particular. Unfortunately, you do not exhibit a financial predisposition that inclines us to believe your potential academic achievements will outweigh the burden of immigration costs as outlined in condition 2.xx. Therefore, we are denying your application for the XXO9 visa at this time and, summarily, your request for a romantic relationship and residency within the household of Citizen A.

As a scientist, you will understand that love is not a thing quantifiable by intent or potential. You have presented us with a complex equation of mating pairs.

Yes, your claims are proliferated by prolonged virtual interaction with Citizen A. and that virtual interaction has been punctuated by periods of direct physical contact and intimacy, a history that you both no doubt found financially draining and spatially difficult to maintain. Your argument is that this is a demonstration of commitment and, while not infallible, a tangible indication of a bond with qualitative value. This is well articulated in your application but in and of itself indicates an acknowledgement of a failure to meet condition 2.xx. The narratives you and Citizen A have provided seem to suggest a genuine longing for this emotional abstraction of love, but the uncertainty inherent in such a concept to begin with grants us the power and jurisdiction to deny your request in its entirety.

That said, considering your purposed research regarding the demodous rotundus, we would like to offer you the standard six-month FU2 tourist visa. No funding for the project should in any way be distributed towards said research, and the FU2 visa prohibits employment of any kind, but we can still see how your research might benefit our interests. You are therefore invited to attempt to pursue a perceived chance at the abstract concept of love at your own financial detriment.

Please take comfort in the fact that theorists have argued that for love to exist there must be a necessary leap of faith which is, by nature, both unreasonable and unquantifiable. Faith being the antithesis of reason, as each demands the other be cast aside in their own favour. Therefore, your love is only a real problem for you to quantify should you admit to it. This is, of course, of no news to you, but that is the logic that lies at the heart of our decision. You might indeed find useful your own study of the sanguivorous demodous rotundus at this titular time.

As you stated in your proposal: draculin, present in the saliva of Vampire bats, acts as an anti-coagulant, keeping the blood from clotting so that the bat might continue to feed. Might we think of your proposed attempts to maintain a relationship with Citizen A similarly? Your energy, should you both chose to continue to expend it, creates a two-way circuit from which neither of you truly benefit. Suppose we had granted the XXO9 visa, and you were to enter Country 1, taking up residence with Citizen A. Your financial history and the financial history of Citizen A indicate that in order to be able to pay rent and buy groceries, you are going to need to take up a second part-time job. Your research — that which enables any visa and is arguably the only harvestable capital that having you in our country creates — will likely suffer in the face of this other commitment. Should you wish to try and skirt the work stipulations of the visa or enter into this country by way of marriage, we would like to remind you that it is this same office that shall determine the emotional validity of that marriage. If deemed invalid, both illegal employment and marriage for visa are jailable and deportable offences. Not to mention the pressure an unprepared marriage would put on both you and Citizen A.

Your application states that you are still under forty. Perhaps you will find it comforting to know that even in the face of this rejection you do have a good amount of your life left to plan and there are, while arguably more expensive, still other chiropterology programs in your own country. We in no way object to you continuing to visit Country 1 throughout the remainder of your prime working years for our benefit, taking the necessary lapses in pay and employment until you become destitute while still paying the dues for recurring FU2 tourist visas. We wish you and Citizen A all the best in attempting to pursue any form of a future together. Or perhaps you might be able to find someone in your own country who wants you.

Sincerely,

Desmond A. Tinderbatratus, Associate Director

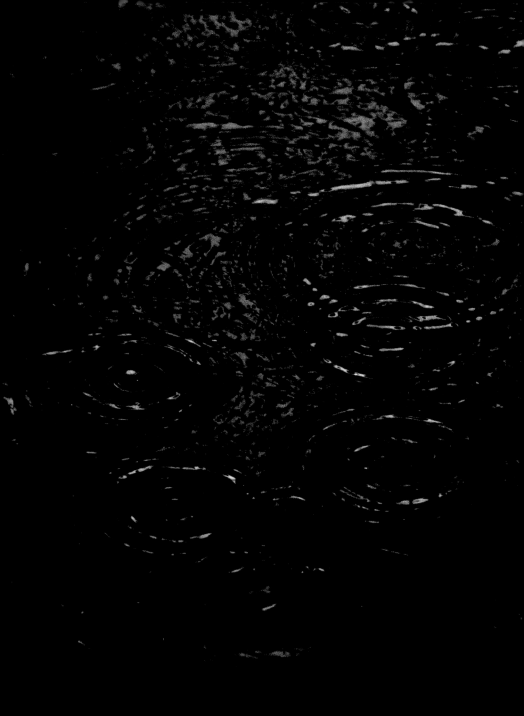

after the circus left town

music faded, tents folded,
posters peeling from the fences
as cheap glue flakes away.
Well-trodden grounds, redolent
of animal droppings
and spun sugar, lie quiet.
Only a small book remains,
dropped, forgotten,
half-trampled into the earth,
bearing among its pages
the seeds of future wonders.

Suzanna Lundale

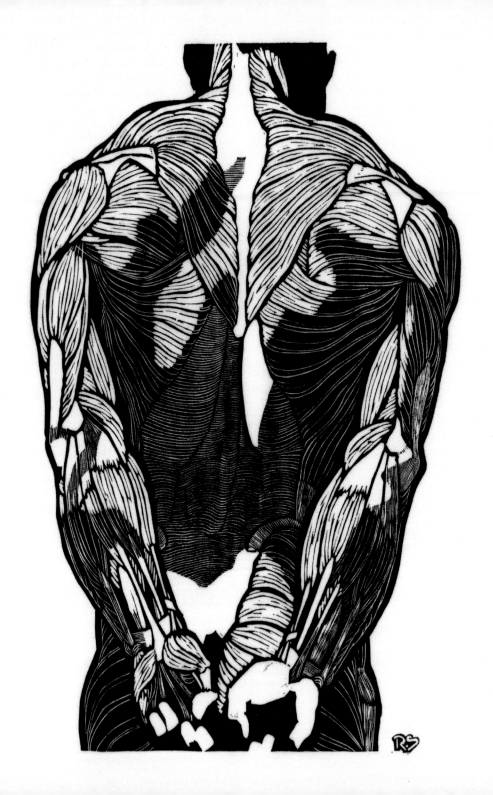

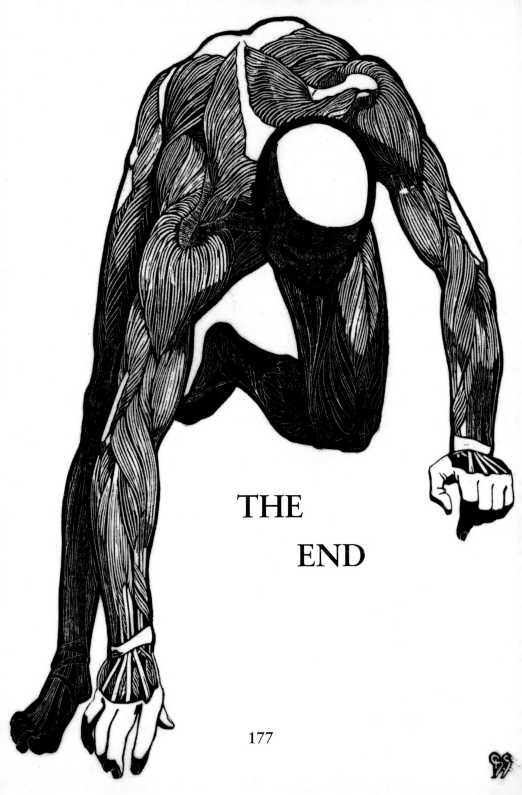

THE

END

✳ THE GOAT ✳

THE GOAT

Contributors

Julian Harvard is a London based writer and screenwriter. He is currently completing a Masters in creative writing at Glasgow University.

Twitter: @JulianHarvard

Michael Ndubuisi Agugom is a recipient of the Iceland Writers Retreat Alumni Award and an MFA candidate at Texas State University. His works have appeared in Prairie Schooner, The Cantabrigian Magazine, and other places. He's the Field-Notes Editor at Porter House Review.

Alex Kanevsky was born in Soviet Union in 1963. He studied mathematics at Vilnius University in Lithuania before coming to the United States. Alex Kanevsky lives and works in New Hampshire. His work is represented by Hollis Taggart in New York and Dolby Chadwick Gallery in San Francisco.

Madeline Docherty is a writer, postgraduate student and communications worker living in Glasgow. Her creative work deals with reproductive illness, gender and labels. An extract of her novel, Gender Theory, recently won the North Lit Agency Prize.

Duncan Richardson's fiction, poetry and history has appeared in various magazines and books, including Subtropical Suspense and Futurevisions. He writes fulltime in Brisbane, Australia has also published a history of Brisbane's worst year, Year of Disaster-Brisbane 1864.

John Sweet writes as a coping mechanism to help him navigate this New Dark Age of the 21st century. Previous collections of his work include Bastard Faith and Brave Retreat. He is extremely honored to be in the vanguard of artists published by the literary juggernaut that is Goatshed Press.

Leonard Baggs has realised his lifelong dream of working on the railways. He has now laid over four hundred miles of track up many hills and down many valleys. Sometimes, when insomnia strikes, he finds himself writing short stories.

Werner Galow is an arist from Cologne. His work has featured in Art Gallerys and various publications. He is inspired by comics, movies, news and books.

Douglas Colston has travelled the world and knows there is no place like home. His poetry, fiction and nonfiction has been published in online and traditional print magazines and anthologies.

Ryan J.M Tan is a Malaysian writer residing in Kuala Lumpur. He studied law but chose not to go down that path. During his free time you can find him watching horror films (with eyes shut), playing the piano (to an audience of one beagle), and baking (usually edible) bread.

Chloe Utting is a 24-year-old poet and writer. She has her BA in American Literature with Creative Writing from the University of East Anglia and is working towards an MA in Creative Writing with the Open University. Her writing focuses on exploring the impact of climate change and destigmatising mental health.

Eduard Tolos Palau is a sculptor from Barcelona. His work is found under the moniker Kabba the Invisible Rainbow.

Abuchi Modilim is the winner of the 2021 Arojah Students Playwriting Prize. His writing has appeared in No Tokens Journal, Jellyfish Review, Abandon Journal, Samjoko Magazine, and is forthcoming in Native Skin and elsewhere. Currently, he is studying English and literary studies with a minor in Theatre and film studies, at the University of Nigeria, Nsukka.

Colleen Anderson's writing has appeared in five countries in such venues as nEvermore!, Shadow Atlas, Amazing and Heroic Fantasy Quarterly. She is a multiple award nominee. Her poetry collection I Dreamed a World is available from LVP Publications, and fiction in A Body of Work (Black Shuck Books) online.

Gabriel Awuah Mainoo is a Ghanaian writer, poet & lyricist. Winner of the 2021 Africa Haiku Prize, Singapore Poetry Prize, the LFP/RML/Library of Africa and the African Diaspora chapbook prize. His writings have appeared in Wales Haiku Journal, EVENT, aAh! Magazine, Prairie Fire, Best New African Poets Anthologies (2018, 2019, 2020).

Philip Webb Gregg writes odd things for beautiful places. Most of his work revolves around the disconnect between human nature and nature nature. He is an editor for the Dark Mountain Project and makes his living as a general scribbler. He's having a very fine day, thank you for asking. philipwebbgregg.com

Naadia A. Hussein is a final year Creative Writing student at the University of Birmingham. She is a passionate writer who recognises the importance of bringing a voice to people and situations often ignored. Dabbling in mediums from poetry to picturebooks, Naadia aims to promote empathy, reassurance and understanding through her work.

Philip Davison lives in Dublin. He has published nine novels. Quiet City is his most recent work. He writes radio drama. He has written two television dramas and one stage play. He co-wrote Learning Gravity, a BBC Storyville documentary on poet and undertaker, Thomas Lynch. His poems have appeared in various journals.

Ed Ahern resumed writing after forty odd years in foreign intelligence and international sales. He's had almost four hundred stories and poems published so far, and six books. Ed works the other side of writing at Bewildering Stories, where he sits on the review board and manages a posse of nine review editors. He's also lead editor at The Scribes Micro Fiction magazine.

Isabel Álvarez is a painter and librarian who lives in North London. She is from the Sierra Nevada, in Andalucia, and her work is the product of a restless and neurotic mind.

Mirri Glasson-Darling lives and writes in Glasgow, Scotland where she moved from Alaska. This year she received a Notable Mention in Best American Essays, has received a Pushcart nomination for short fiction, and work of hers has appeared in the Colorado Review as well as other literary magazines.

Suzanna Lundale is a writer & globe-trotter passionate about storytelling, history, travel, & the people – real & imagined - populating her galaxy. Her dual heritage, Latinx/Scandinavian-American, actively informs the complexity of her worldview and fascination with questions of identity and liminal spaces. She tweets poetry & fictional vignettes as @ SuzannaLundale.

Want to contact any of our writers? Email us at goatshedpress.co.uk and we will pass on any (nice) messages.

Meet The Team

Jack Jenkins — Editor and Co-Founder

Jack has worked various publishing jobs in addition to special needs teaching and physiotherapy. He is hard at work on his debut novel, Catwalk Through Bedlam, a black comedy thriller set in Bristol.

David Humphries — Designer and Co-founder

David worked in advertising and marketing for many years, where he was awarded Drinks Launch of the Year 1981. Recently, he has retired in order to focus on his love of art and literature, and leads the design wing of Goatshed Press.

Gabriel Awuah Mainoo — Poetry Editor

Gabriel is a Ghanaian editor & author of five books. He edits poetry for Better Than Starbucks Poetry & Fiction Journal, Ghana Writes Journal and WGM Magazine. He's a freelance poetry editor at Valley Press, UK.

Anna Hughes — Fiction Editor and Proofreader

Anna is a gynecologist and obstertrician based in London. She works as a freelance editor and literary advisor. Anna is currently working on her long-time ambition of opening a bookshop with beds and sofas, where people can eat, drink, sleep and, of course, read.

Eager for more?

Introducing Goatshed Pocket Books, collections of
poetry, prose and essays, soon to be available on
goatshedpress.co.uk and in bookshops around the world.